THE CONFESSIONS OF POPE JOAN

VATICAN SECRET ARCHIVE THRILLERS
BOOK SEVEN

GARY MCAVOY

LITERATI
EDITIONS.

Hardcover ISBN: 978-1-954123-38-0
Paperback ISBN: 978-1-954123-37-3
eBook ISBN: 978-1-954123-36-6

Library of Congress Control Number: 2023912289

Published by:
Literati Editions
PO Box 5987
Bremerton WA 98312-5987
Email: info@LiteratiEditions.com
Visit the author's website: www.GaryMcAvoy.com

This is a work of fiction. Names, characters, businesses, places, long-standing institutions, agencies, public offices, events, locales and incidents are either the products of the author's imagination or have been used in a fictitious manner. Apart from historical references, any resemblance to actual persons, living or dead, or actual events is purely coincidental.

BOOKS BY GARY MCAVOY

FICTION

The Confessions of Pope Joan

The Galileo Gambit

The Jerusalem Scrolls

The Avignon Affair

The Petrus Prophecy

The Opus Dictum

The Vivaldi Cipher

The Magdalene Veil

The Magdalene Reliquary

The Magdalene Deception

NONFICTION

And Every Word Is True

PROLOGUE

ROME, ITALY – 857 CE

As the legend goes, the *sedia gestatoria*—a litter supporting the portable, red velvet papal chair adorned with flowers and garlands—was carried along the uneven cobblestone streets on the shoulders of the faithful *palafrenieri*, an elite group of Italian nobles in service to the Holy Father. The cheering crowds along the route gave way as the Easter procession of Pope John VIII and his entourage made its way up the Caelian Hill and on to the Lateran Palace, sanctuary of the papal residence and Apostolic offices.

The streets were lined with shops and market stalls selling everything from food and clothing to household goods and luxury items. The smell of roasting beef, freshly baked bread and aromatic spices filled the air, along with the pungent odor of animals, since vendors kept livestock close to their stalls, allowing them to ensure the freshness of their products, demonstrate their quality, and advertise their goods effectively to customers looking to purchase fresh meats slaughtered on site.

The *palafrenieri* had just guided the papal carriage through the Roman Forum and onto the famed Via Sacra when suddenly the pope frantically motioned for his entourage to stop and allow him to step down off the platform. The adoring throng surrounding him assumed he was stopping to embrace them and to give them his blessing. But that was not to be.

The pope stepped down, his face twisted in anguish, and inexplicably began to mount one of the ceremonial horses prancing astride the procession, presumably to take off for someplace more quickly than the *palafrenieri* were able to take him on foot.

But his attempted mounting failed, and he stumbled off the horse and down onto the cold cobblestones. Now wailing in pain, the pope lay down on his back, lifted his knees and spread his legs, pulled up his gown and, mere moments later—to the shock and horror of onlookers—the crowning of an infant's head appeared from his nether region, followed immediately by the tiny body of a newborn boy.

IOHANNES·PAPA

The people, not understanding what was happening, were thoroughly confused. *Why had the Holy Father hidden an infant beneath his vestments?* they wondered. *What was this curious vexation?*

But then they witnessed the blood, the gush of amniotic fluids onto the cobbles, then the dark red placenta fell out, along with the umbilical cord attached to the child.

Word spread quickly through the assembled crowd that Pope John's gender was not that of a man at all, but of a woman! *A female pope?!* they murmured. *The very thought was preposterous!*

Angered by the obviously willful deceit, or worse, that this was the unholy work of witchcraft or even Satan, people began throwing stones at the pope and her child. Papal guards—who were as surprised as anyone—were still bound by their sacred duties and took the pope and her child under their wings, whisking them back onto the litter and, in pell-mell fashion, raced as fast as the feet of the *palafrenieri* could carry them further up the hill and into the safety of the Lateran Palace.

Consequently, the papacy of "Pope Joan" was short-lived and shrouded in mystery, leading many to later believe that she never existed. The disgrace and humiliation it would bring to the Church should she be found a legitimate pope would be too great to bear, so for centuries the Church had shrouded her factual existence to that of being a fanciful myth, a sham legend, relegating it to being purely a falsehood by the centuries-old Order of Papal Guardians, a league of European nobles who to this day rejected the concept of Joan's legitimacy as pope.

~

MANY YEARS EARLIER

In the ninth century, England was divided into a number of different kingdoms, with the most powerful being the Kingdom of Wessex, ruled by the Anglo-Saxon king Alfred the Great. During this period, the relationship between England and the Vatican was shaped by a number of different factors, including politics, religion, and warfare—but perhaps none as impactful as the arrival of St. Augustine of Canterbury in 597.

Sent by Pope Gregory the Great, Augustine's primary mission was to convert the Anglo-Saxons to Christianity, a mission that heralded the beginning of a transformative epoch in England's history—its Christianization. As the Christian faith took root and grew over the centuries that followed, so too did the influence and power of the Catholic Church in England.

St. Augustine of Canterbury's arrival marked a major shift in the religious and social dynamics of England. Previously a largely pagan society, England was swept by a wave of Christian teachings and beliefs that were gradually assimilated into its social fabric. St. Augustine himself established the Archbishopric of Canterbury, becoming its first archbishop and paving the way for the central role this institution would play in England's religious, and subsequently political, life. The archbishopric would later act as a crucial bridge between the English crown and the Vatican, further intensifying their relationship.

The spread of Christianity in England wasn't seamless. As the Catholic Church extended its influence, it found itself in conflict with various elements of society, both domestically and abroad. One of the most significant external challenges to the growing Church came with the Viking invasions that began in the late eighth century and persisted throughout the ninth. These invasions marked a time of intense struggle for the Catholic Church and England as a whole.

The Vikings, originating from Scandinavia, were predominantly pagan, and they posed a substantial threat to the burgeoning Christian establishment. Their frequent attacks targeted Christian monasteries and churches, the symbols of the new faith, and the repositories of valuable religious artifacts and literate clergy. The assaults on these monastic sites not only resulted in physical destruction but also threatened the dissemination of Christian learning and culture that these institutions nurtured. Moreover, the Vikings' disregard for the sanctity of these religious sites challenged the authority of the Church and the monarchy that protected it, forcing them to develop new strategies to secure their positions.

These violent conflicts, however, weren't merely destructive. The Catholic Church, monarchy, and general population were forced to consolidate their beliefs and strengthen their defenses, thereby promoting a stronger sense of community and shared identity. This process ultimately contributed to the development of a more unified English nation under a Christian banner, further embedding the influence of the Catholic Church in the political and social life of the country.

As the Viking invasions tapered off towards the end of the ninth century, the Catholic Church, having weathered the storm, emerged more entrenched than before with the English monarchy. This relationship would continue to evolve over the ensuing centuries, marked by a series of political and military conflicts, forming a complex and intertwined history between the Catholic Church and the English monarchy.

LIKELY SEEKING to evade the Viking incursions while bringing their message of Christianity to the European continent, the English missionary parents of Johanna, or Joan, Anglicus had moved from their ancestral home of Sherborne, England, to the fertile conversion grounds of Mainz, Germany, where Joan was born in 815.

Despite her humble origins growing up on a small farm, Joan had prepared herself well in life. An ambitious young girl, she developed an unquenchable thirst for knowledge and languages, both of which she ultimately mastered through as much schooling as was permitted women in the early ninth century, as well as by reading every book she could lay her hands on. In her teen years, she found furtive refuge in the local libraries of monasteries and institutions of learning, becoming proficient in Latin, Greek and German.

But the best educational opportunities were available only to men—men whose ambitions were to lead the world in all manner of occupations: educators and doctors, shipbuilders and shop merchants, and the more humble but essential vocations such as farmers, butchers, and carpenters, as well as those called to religious life.

Joan realized early on that to fulfill her desires to learn all there was to know, the norm would have to be different for her. The life of an uneducated woman doing what was expected of women became unthinkable to her. She wanted far more out of life—but to do that, she would have to take drastic measures.

Among the top schools of learning in Germany at the time was the Benedictine's Fulda Monastery, where more than anything Joan wished to study. But she knew that, as a girl, she would never be permitted enrollment or even visiting status at a monastic school.

One day as she was walking along a familiar road, she encountered a young monk from the Fulda Monastery with whom she struck up a friendship. Sympathetic to her desire to learn, over time the monk had smuggled out various books and manuscripts from the monastery's vast library for her to read. Her educational aptitude was insatiable; she simply could not gain enough knowledge and, in time, became quite learned, improving her languages with earnest fluency and impressing those she encountered in all walks of life, who were surprised that a mere girl could know so much.

But Joan still deeply desired a more formal education, and in time, she and the monk hatched a plan for her to change her appearance to that of a boy, thus enabling her to at least be considered by the abbot for enrollment. Her hair was cut and shaped as a boy's, and she adapted the deeper voice and more masculine gait of her male counterparts. The monk even provided her with one of his own brown, hooded woolen habits to mask her feminine features. And not long after, he introduced Joan to his superior at Fulda Monastery, Abbot Rabanus Maurus, as a childhood friend named "John" Anglicus.

Abbot Maurus was duly impressed with this new candidate for his monastic order, especially the "boy's" remarkable facility in three languages at such a young age, an aptitude upon which the Benedictines were at the time placing great emphasis in expanding their mission.

And so, in short order, Brother John Anglicus took his probationary monastic vows as a Benedictine monk. Joan had made it, and as long as she hid her true self—not difficult to do in the sequestration of a chaste and solitary monastery—she would survive well and learn.

As the years went by, such masculine adaptations had become so ingrained in her that, for all intents and purposes, she was recognized and accepted as a man by everyone she encountered.

～

SOMETIME IN HER TWENTIES, Joan was drawn to Athens and the more expansive educational opportunities available there. In the early Middle Ages, Athens was

THE CONFESSIONS OF POPE JOAN

controlled by the Byzantine Empire, and education was primarily focused on the study of classical Greek literature, philosophy, and history. The city attracted scholars and intellectuals throughout the Middle Ages, and Athens remained an important center of learning, with its ancient ruins and monuments continuing to inspire scholarship and intellectual inquiry.

By this time, Joan was successfully passing herself off as an English priest, Father John Anglicus. Her superb education was apparent even to the dimmest of those she encountered, so once again she had carved her way inside the male-dominated institutions of higher learning in Greece. She often spoke at assemblies and became a recognized authority on many topics—a master whom people in high places soon heard of but would not soon forget.

In 847, Joan, now in her early thirties, decided she wanted a deeper connection to the Church in Rome, and left Athens for the Eternal City. Already an accomplished teacher, she sought out and procured opportunities as an educator, orator, and tutor. Eventually word of her scholarship and achievements reached the ears of powerful men in the Church, and Father John Anglicus was soon invited to work inside the historic walls of Vatican City.

As a standout priest gaining broad respect from those with whom she worked and taught, Joan's "Father John" persona had gained such accord that "he" was promoted to Cardinal John Anglicus a mere year later, while serving as personal secretary to Pope Leo IV.

In the heart of the Middle Ages, a profound narrative was unfolding, one that would send shockwaves through the annals of religious history. It was during this period that Joan, a woman of unparalleled intellect and charisma, was believed to have made a revelation that was as daring as it was unthinkable: She had taken on a lover.

The whispers around the Vatican corridors suggested that Joan's paramour was not just any man within the confines of the Holy City but an influential cardinal. This man was believed to not only be aware of Joan's audacious masquerade, as a woman concealed within the vestments of a man, but he had actively nurtured and promoted it. The tale of their relationship was shrouded in a layer of mystery and intrigue, further fueling the rumors that swirled around the Holy See.

Pope Leo IV, the reigning pontiff of the time, had been suffering from a protracted illness. His health had been in decline, and his days were seemingly numbered. Finally, after a long battle, the pope succumbed to his ailment and passed away, leaving the papal throne vacant and the Curia in a state of anticipation and apprehension.

Joan Anglicus was in an advantageous position during this transition. For nearly three decades, she had maintained her façade, living and working as a man within the walls of the Vatican. Her in-depth knowledge of Church and Curial matters was exceptional, and her intellectual prowess was widely acknowledged. Moreover, her affable nature and ability to navigate the complex webs of ecclesiastical politics had earned her widespread likability among the clergy and laity alike.

These factors, combined with her physical proximity to the papal offices and her alleged relationship with the influential cardinal, created a unique momentum in her favor. With a mix of awe and disbelief, the cardinals gathered in Conclave to elect the successor to St. Peter's

Throne, and Joan Anglicus, the woman who had been masquerading as a man for nearly three decades, was chosen. She ascended to the throne of the Catholic Church under the name of Pope John VIII.

Joan's ascension as Pope was a pivotal moment in the history of the Church, one shrouded in secrecy, intrigue, and scandal. Not only did it represent the culmination of her audacious masquerade, but it also marked a point of intense controversy that has stirred debate among scholars and theologians for centuries, unraveling a narrative that continues to fascinate and confound all who plunge into the Vatican's labyrinthine past.

CHAPTER
ONE
PRESENT DAY

I t was a warm Monday morning in May at the John Felice Rome Center, a Jesuit subsidiary campus of Loyola University Chicago not far from Vatican City. Having just taken his first official teaching job at the Rome Center, young Robert Anglicus was leading his maiden class in medieval studies for the esteemed academy's summer session.

As he began, his voice betrayed his nervousness as he dug into the gist of his introduction.

"Okay... well, the, uh, Middle Ages, also known as the medieval period, was a time of great political and social change in Europe. It was a period of transition between the ancient world and the modern era, and it saw the rise and fall of great empires, advances in architecture, art, and literature, trade and commerce, and the development of new systems of government and society..." As he continued, he ambled up and down the aisles between desk rows, as much to keep moving to relieve his mild anxiety as to better engage with his students.

"During this time, the Catholic Church was a dominant force in Europe, shaping both religious and secular life, while feudalism provided the social and economic framework for much of society. The Church was also the primary source of education at the time. Monks and nuns were responsible for preserving ancient texts and knowledge, and they taught literacy and numeracy to those who sought it. The Church played a vital role in social organization as well. It provided a sense of community, support, and charity to people who were vulnerable, such as widows and orphans. It also offered guidance on marriage and family life, as well as regulating moral behavior. Even in politics, bishops and other Church officials had major influence in the governance of local communities, and the Church played a fundamental role in the coronation of kings and queens.

"By understanding the complexities and nuances of this period, we can gain insight into the origins of many of the political, social, and cultural institutions that still shape our world today..." And on he continued.

Despite first day jitters, he felt it was a fine opening lecture, and his unease lessened as he found his ground and observed his students paying rapt attention, each of whom had worked hard to earn a coveted spot in the prestigious international school.

At thirty-one years of age, Robbie Anglicus was the youngest professor on campus, a fact that drew some derision from the older, stodgier faculty but welcome praise from the more progressive academic staff and students who could better relate to a younger, more liberally enlightened teacher. Robbie had been encouraged to apply for the position by his close friend and fellow Loyola alumnus Dr. Aaron Pearce, who himself had only been teaching at the Rome Center since the fall semester.

Originally from London, Robbie was a striking and engaging Englishman from a once aristocratic family with ancient roots in Wessex. He sported long, curly blond hair cresting clear blue eyes on an angular face atop a fit, six-foot frame. Like Aaron, he was an avid lacrosse player, and once he'd adjusted to life on campus, was intent on joining one of the local teams that frequently gathered on the campus's Loyola Ramblers lacrosse field for practice and competitive tourneys.

CUGINA BAR WAS NESTLED in the back alley off a main avenue near the John Felice Rome Center campus, a place where many students and younger faculty met up after classes to toss back a beer or two. Its atmosphere had a cool vibe to it, with light jazz playing softly in the background and Italian Renaissance reproductions hanging on high, pale yellow walls.

Aaron, Father Michael Dominic from the Vatican, and *Le Monde* journalist Hana Sinclair had already entered the bar when Robbie strode in and waved to Aaron.

"I've heard so much about both of you from this one," Robbie addressed Michael and Hana as he motioned to Aaron with his thumb. "It is a pleasure to finally meet the lovely Hana. Aaron has told me so much about you."

Hana looked at Aaron askance and he grinned in

return. It was clear Aaron had mentioned their dating to his good friend. And that Hana was a bit surprised at the mention of it.

Robbie quickly turned to Michael. "And it's like I know you already. He's got to be one of your biggest fans."

"As I'm one of his," Father Michael beamed, standing to grip Aaron's shoulder in a bonding show of friendship. Notwithstanding Robbie's sense of knowing them, Aaron made quick formal introductions, then as they sat, Michael asked, "So, how are you liking it here so far, Robbie? Settling in over at the Rome Center yet?"

"I've only been here a week and my first classes kicked off today, so I confess to being a bit nervous. I always get a little stage fright at first, especially when I don't yet know people. But once I get talking passionately about medieval history, I find my ground pretty quickly. I'm sure it's that staid British upbringing that accounts for my shyness." He laughed self-consciously.

Michael raised his bottle of beer toward Robbie in a gesture of support. "I had the same problem of impostor syndrome in my immediate post-seminary days, feeling like a fraud as a brand-new priest. But one trick is to focus on others. Instead of leaning on your own self-consciousness, try transferring attention to others and their needs. Trust me, this can help a lot in reducing any inhibitions you might have."

Robbie looked at Michael with optimism. "That's good advice, Michael, thanks. I've never thought about shifting attention onto others, but I can see how that might work. So, what is it you do at the Vatican?"

Everyone laughed. "Nice segue, Robbie," Hana said. "You're learning already."

Michael answered, "I'm prefect of the Apostolic Archives, or what you might know as the Secret Archives. I've been there for, oh, going on four years now. And I love that you're passionate about medieval history, something we both share. I deal with it daily in the millions of manuscripts we care for, and I couldn't love any job more."

"Wow! I can't think of a cooler place to be than as head custodian for history's greatest collection of the written word! I can only imagine the amazing things you must have buried there."

"That's actually one of our problems. I literally have to 'imagine' much of it as well, since the vast majority of our holdings have never been seen by anyone living nor catalogued by anyone who came before me. So there's really no telling what's to be found in there, apart from the tiny fraction that has already been indexed."

The beer was loosening Michael's tongue, and now he was on a roll. "To illustrate the challenges we face, here's just one example. Apart from the millions of documents stored on over fifty miles of shelf space, we have these beautiful, enormous oak cabinets from the Borghese period, fifteen of them called *armadios*, each filled with some ten thousand packets of material. In order to document the items within *one single packet* from one cabinet, two experts would need to dedicate their full time to the task continuously for one week. At that rate, to index all ten thousand packages in just a single cabinet would take almost two hundred years! And remember, there are fifteen cabinets, which represent just a tiny fraction of the Archives."

"Good God," Robbie marveled. "That must drive you crazy, not knowing what important historical treasures might be hidden there just waiting to be found. The oldest artifact I've ever seen is our own family Bible, which was passed down through our family by a long distant relative: Æthelbald, King of Wessex in the ninth century."

Michael's face abruptly took on a contemplative look, as if trying to recall a forgotten memory.

"What did you say your last name was, Robbie?" he asked.

"Anglicus. Our family can be traced back at least a thousand years."

At once, Michael's demeanor turned to awestruck. "Anglicus… as in Codex Anglicus? Your family wouldn't happen to know who owns the Codex Anglicus, would you?"

"You've heard of it?" Robbie said, his mouth agape. "That's my family's bible."

"*Heard* of it?!" Michael replied with equal astonishment. "As a true copy of the Codex Vaticanus, one of the oldest surviving copies of the Bible, it's legendary! At least it is among book nerds like me. The Codex Vaticanus is held in high regard by biblical scholars for its scriptural accuracy, and the fact that it was written shortly after the death of Jesus, relatively speaking. And your family's Bible, the Codex Anglicus, was commissioned by King Æthelbald as a faithful reproduction of that fourth-century Codex Vaticanus, translated from the Greek into Old English by command of the king, with the cooperation of Pope John VIII in 855. Gosh, I'd love to see it sometime, Robbie."

"You're welcome any time, Michael."

"Speaking of which… As it happens, I'm scheduled to go to London next weekend to assist in final planning for an important exhibition between the British Museum and the Vatican. Would that be too soon?"

"Not at all!" Robbie said, enthused. "The school has a mid-term break coming up next week, so Aaron and I have the time. And you should all come. We've got plenty of room at the house, and we'll make a jolly good time of it. And though they already know Aaron, my parents would love to meet all of you. They worry that my shyness inhibits me from making new acquaintances."

"I'm up for a quick trip to England," Hana said, raising her hand. "Where's your family home located, Robbie?"

"Saxon Hall is in Wessex—Dorset, actually—on the fringe of a little village called Shillingstone."

"'Saxon Hall' sounds terribly posh," Hana noted. "Is it one of those grand old English country estates?"

"Exactly right," Robbie said, grinning as he raked back his blond curls. "It was built in the sixteenth century, but mum and dad have remodeled it endlessly. It's quite comfortable. I'm sure you'll enjoy yourselves. We can fly into Bournemouth Airport where Cedric, our family driver, will pick us up."

Glancing at Michael, Hana raised her eyebrows. "This is going to be great fun."

"You're telling me. The Codex Anglicus is one of those rarities few people have ever seen. I knew it was in private hands, just not whose. What great luck! And I'll bet it's in spectacular condition."

"Yes, it is," Robbie confirmed. "You'll be surprised how fresh it looks, replete with full color illustrations. It is the pride of our family."

"As well it should be," Michael agreed. "Okay, it's a date then."

CHAPTER

TWO

It was Saturday morning, and the three-hour Ryanair flight from Rome to Bournemouth, England, was pleasant enough, with Michael and Hana playing gin rummy on their tray tables while Aaron took a nap and Robbie read a book.

As the jet neared its destination, the playful Irish brogue of a male flight attendant's voice came on over the PA system: "Ladies and gentlemen, as we start our descent, please return your seats to their upright and most uncomfortable position. Keep your seat belts fastened and please try to enjoy our complimentary turbulence. Since we will be flying over water, your seat cushions can be used as flotation devices, so in the event of an emergency water landing, please take one with our compliments at no additional charge. And finally, we'll be landing as soon as we get closer to the ground."

Michael, Hana, and the rest of the passengers all had a good laugh, after which Hana gathered up all the cards and declared, "I win. As usual."

"Whaddya mean, 'as usual'?" Michael said, feigning indignation.

"So, when are you heading to London and the British Museum? I'd love to tag along, if that's okay."

Michael laughed. "That's right, change the subject… Well, it's a bank holiday weekend, so I'll probably head out on Tuesday, and of course you're welcome to join me. Maybe the others might like to come as well."

"So, what's this exhibition all about?" she asked. "I know you've been working on it for the past year or so."

"It's quite an extraordinary event," he said, his eyes shimmering with anticipation. "Two esteemed institutions, the British Museum and the Vatican Apostolic Archives, will come together to present a historic collection of Church artifacts. We've titled it *Echoes of Faith*."

Hana's interest was piqued. "*Echoes of Faith*?" she echoed, "That sounds profound."

Michael chuckled softly. "Indeed, it is. The title perfectly abbreviates the intent behind the exhibition. It seeks to present the historic resonance of the Church's legacy, echoing down through centuries. A symphony of faith, if you will."

Hana leaned forward, her eagerness to understand more was infectious. Michael continued, "The exhibition is broken into several parts. The first, 'The Scribes of God', will display invaluable manuscripts from the Vatican Archives, some dating back to the early Christian Era. You'll find the Codex Vaticanus there, one of the oldest known copies of the Greek Bible and the inspiration for Robbie's own Codex Anglicus. It is thought to be one of the most faithful translations of a Greek Bible in the form that it existed at that time."

"Well," exclaimed Hana, "that's timely relevance."

"The exhibition takes a deeper dive into history with 'Relics: Tangible Echoes of Saints'. Visitors will be able to see the Shard of the True Cross and even a thorn believed to be from Christ's Crown of Thorns."

Hana was silent, absorbing the gravity of what Michael was saying. "And there's more," he added. "Sections dedicated to the art of vestments and liturgical objects, an exploration of sacred art and sculpture, and a walk through different papal eras."

Hana's gaze held a newfound respect, "It's not *just* an exhibition, then, is it?"

Michael shook his head, a soft smile playing on his lips. "No, not at all. It's a journey, a pilgrimage through time and faith. It's history coming alive, stories echoing from artifacts, reminding us of the vast ocean of devotion that the Church has sailed through. It's about feeling connected to the past, drawing lessons from it, and finding inspiration."

Hana sat back, quiet and reflective. "Well, you've got my attention," she finally said, her voice filled with reverence. "I can't wait to experience it, Michael." The priest simply nodded, pleased to see the flame of curiosity burn brighter in her eyes, especially knowing her to be an agnostic. "It's my pleasure, Hana. After all, knowledge shared deepens its value."

Michael reached across the aisle and tapped Aaron awake from his slumber. "Hey, buddy, we're about to land."

Aaron's eyes slowly opened and he yawned, reaching both arms forward to stretch. "Gosh, I could sleep another couple of hours. Maybe I can get another nap in at Robbie's place."

. . .

THEIR CARRY-ON BAGS COLLECTED, they all made their way to the passenger pickup zone, where Robbie said their car would be waiting. And sure enough, it was: a stunning, vintage 1968 Rolls-Royce Phantom V. The chauffeur was standing next to the car, and when he saw Robbie, he allowed a discreet smile.

"Hello, Cedric!" Robbie said. "Good to see you again. And thanks so much for picking us up."

"With pleasure, Master Robbie, and welcome home. I'll take those, if you don't mind." Reaching for the bags, Cedric stowed everything neatly in the boot of the Rolls.

"Directly home, sir? Or did you wish to stop somewhere along the way?"

"Just take us to the house, Cedric, thanks."

THE CHARMING HILLS and valleys of the English countryside drifted past as the Phantom made its way through Wessex to Dorset, passing such landmarks as the picturesque village of Lulworth Cove, with its soaring seventeenth-century Lulworth Castle, a four-story, white-stone behemoth set back on a sprawling and meticulously maintained carpet of green lawn. One could imagine batteries of archers at the top of its crenellated towers, valiantly defending the castle from the Viking marauders of an earlier age.

"It's been some time since I've been out here on the English lowlands," Michael remarked as he stared through the window, taking in the passing sights. "It's such an incredibly historic place."

"Given what you know, what impresses you most about it?" Hana asked.

"Well, at its height—in the late nineteenth and early

twentieth centuries—the British Empire was the largest and most influential force in the world, spanning over a quarter of the world's land area and ruling over nearly a quarter of the world's population. Just think about that— a *fourth* of the entire world's land and population..." He allowed the image to settle in everyone's mind before continuing.

"The British Empire's economic, military, and political power was unparalleled, and it had a profound impact on the whole world during its existence. Its vast network of colonies and territories allowed Britain to control the world's major trade routes and dominate the entire global economy. And the British navy was the most powerful in the world, giving Britain the ability to project its military might across the globe.

"But its influence extended well beyond its economic and military powers. It also had a significant impact on culture, language, and social norms. The English language, for example, spread widely throughout the Empire and, as a direct result, remains one of the most widely spoken languages in the world today. The Empire's influence on literature, music, and art was also important, with many artists and writers drawing inspiration from the diverse cultures and peoples that the Empire encompassed. At one point and for some time, British rule extended over Canada, India, Australia, most of the African continent including Egypt and Sudan, Singapore and Hong Kong, Jamaica and the Bahamas, Malta... the list goes on. You just can't imagine Great Britain's impact on the world, though of course things are much different now, largely eclipsed by the United States as the reigning economic and military superpower."

"Well, now that you put it that way," Hana said, "I can see why you're impressed."

"Ah, we're here," Robbie said as the Rolls-Royce turned onto a long, paved drive bordered by thick gnarled oak trees, their joined canopies arching over the long black snout of the car as if it were driving through an endless leafy tunnel. Looming in the distance ahead through the foggy gray mist lay Saxon Hall, a breathtaking, three-story, 16th-century manor house on a 2000-hectare estate.

"Well, Robbie!" Hana marveled. "You failed to mention how magnificent this place is. How many rooms does it have?"

"Hmm. I'm not quite sure, actually. But I do know it has fourteen bedrooms and I think eighteen loos. And there's a stable round back for the horses. My father favors the occasional fox hunt."

"Of course he does," Hana said wryly, smiling at Aaron with a feigned arched brow.

Pulling up to the entry of the grand home, Cedric gradually brought the Phantom to a slow and gentle halt, at which point doors were flung open and the four passengers emerged.

"You will find the luggage in your rooms," the chauffeur said stoically as he hoisted the few bags out of the car's boot. "I believe Miss Charlotte will advise you on your room assignments."

"Charlotte is the head housekeeper," Robbie noted, "and she's a real busybody, so do be on your best behavior." He smiled impishly as he led the others through the main entrance and into an enormous foyer, with two grand staircases, one on either side of a wide hallway receding into the depths of the house. A shimmering crystal chandelier hung over the hall, its prismatic light casting flashes of rainbows throughout the space.

"This is an altogether warm and welcoming home, Robbie," Hana said. "If I'm not being rude, is your family's wealth generational, or…?"

"Wealth?! Goodness no, we're not wealthy by any means. The house does have a small trust left by our ancestors for its care, but it's all my parents can do to keep things in running order. Many English estates with historic homes and large landholdings like ours face similar financial challenges, such as the high cost of maintaining and restoring aging buildings, high property taxes, and the limited income opportunities available from traditional estate activities like agriculture and forestry.

"My father is a barrister, but while he does make a decent living, everything goes into preserving the estate's heritage. We're not alone, of course. Many such properties face the same pressure, one reason so many of them are now open to the public. An estate that's open to the public for at least twenty-eight days a year is usually eligible for business rates tax relief. Mum doesn't want people traipsing through her house, though, so for us, that's not an option."

Just then an attractive, well-dressed woman descended one of the staircases, a welcoming smile directed at her arriving guests. Robbie met her at the base of the stairs and gave her a kiss on the cheek.

"Hello, Mum. You're looking marvelous today. I'd like to introduce you to my friends. Everyone, this is my mother, Victoria." Robbie then went around, presenting each person by name as his mother greeted them with a firm handshake. When Michael's turn came, Victoria asked, "Catholic or Church of England?"

Michael smiled. "Catholic, I'm afraid!" Both of them laughed.

"All faiths are welcome in Saxon Hall, Father Dominic. You must see our chapel while you're here."

"I'd love to, Victoria, thank you. But I'm especially keen on having a look at that Codex Anglicus Robbie mentioned. I'm a bit of a book nut, you see. Especially when it comes to ancient bibles."

"Father Dominic is in charge of the Vatican Secret Archives, Mum," Robbie said, adding in a stage whisper, "And, he's very close to the pope."

Michael figured he did not need to elaborate just how close he was to the Holy Father, and let that introduction suffice.

"Is that so?" she said, clearly impressed. "Then yes, you must see our Bible after lunch. I'm sure it doesn't compare to the treasures you must see every day, Father, but it is a very special paragon of our own."

"I'm looking forward to it. And please, Victoria, call me Michael."

"Michael it is, then. Well, so lovely to meet you all," she said warmly. "Would you like something to eat or drink? Cook has prepared a buffet of sorts, expecting you might be peckish after your flight." Everyone eagerly agreed. Victoria led them through to the dining room, where a colorful and tempting buffet had been beautifully laid out on a long walnut sideboard.

Not bashful, Aaron led the charge, taking a plate and loading it up. Glancing at the sideboard, he spied a platter of deli meats—roast beef, honey-glazed ham, and turkey slices rolled in a tempting display. Beyond that was a cheese board boasting mature cheddar, creamy Stilton, and a more delicate Brie, accompanied by seedless grapes and small stacks of crackers. A beautifully decorated porcelain bowl contained a classic potato salad, creamy and garnished with chives. Next to that was a mixed greens salad, studded with cherry tomatoes, cucumber slices, and red onions, drizzled with a vinaigrette that caught the light just so.

A freshly baked quiche Lorraine—its flaky crust and creamy, bacon-filled interior steaming slightly—beckoned from a nearby trivet. His eyes caught the gleam of a smoked salmon platter, arranged in elegant folds and decorated with thin lemon wedges and capers. Beside it, a bowl of prawns rested on a bed of crunchy iceberg lettuce, with cocktail sauce served in a separate crystal bowl. It was a perfect representation of English culinary tradition, a tableau of comfort and elegance, with a dash of indulgence.

Aaron having sampled everything onto his plate, the others followed suit and took their places at a sprawling mahogany dining table that seated eighteen, clearly well beyond antique and likely constructed in that very room some centuries earlier, since it was too large to have been moved there.

FOLLOWING LUNCH, Robbie gave them a tour of the great house including showing each of them their rooms. "I understand Charlotte has the day off, so I've got room appointment duty. Hana, I believe this will be yours." A massive four-poster mahogany bed with a soft white laced canopy draped over it was set against the far wall of the ten-meter-long room, with a mirrored dressing table placed between two arched windows overlooking the estate's rolling hills outside.

"What a beautiful suite, Robbie. Can't we all stay here a week or two, Michael? I could get used to this." She offered a playful pout, although they both knew her job as a journalist wouldn't wait for a prolonged vacation and that Michael too would need to get back to his Vatican duties.

"You can do anything you want. But I have the British Museum exhibit coming up..." he chided her. "So, Robbie... Is this a good time to see your family Bible?"

"As good a time as any. It's in the library, follow me." He led them through a series of hallways and passages, as if it were some kind of shortcut through the servant's quarters and service passageways. They ascended a narrow staircase toward the back of the house, which led to a spacious hallway on the second floor with a long, red-patterned Oriental carpet extending some twenty meters, as if it were custom made just for that section of floor.

The two-story library was just as impressive, what one might expect of a proper manor house, boasting thousands of books, with paintings by the Old Masters hung in alcoves between the walnut shelves featuring dark bronze plaques identifying the range of topics for each section. Dominating the room was a colossal antique globe, cradled in an elegant mahogany stand. The orb was an impressive sight, painstakingly hand-painted, displaying the world as it was known centuries ago. Its surfaces were adorned with exquisite calligraphy and mythological sea creatures that navigated around faded outlines of continents, their boundaries significantly different from today's familiar configuration. This terrestrial sphere, a mix of sepia and azure tones, was weathered and faded in spots, but it only added to its charm. An iridescent patina clung to its surface, a testament to its antiquity. It spun smoothly on its axis, a precisely engineered testament to its craftsman, a whispering echo of its original glory.

At the far end of the room was a solid wall of arched windows, facing north so as not to have direct light falling on the fragile books, while providing an excellent naturally soft reading light.

And at the very center of one wall, sitting on its own easel crafted of warm, red cherry with striking grain patterns—was a massive book identical to the Codex Vaticanus, composed of 759 thin vellum pages the color of dried wheat, with wooden boards on front and back inset with very old, intricately carved ivory—which Michael knew was only used on books that were deemed the most valuable in medieval times.

"Extraordinary," he mumbled to himself. He ran his fingers across the inset ivory embellishments and brass clamshell corners, marveling at the book's superb condition for its age.

"In my line of work, I'd only heard legends about the Codex Anglicus, but never knew who actually had possession of it. What a strange coincidence this is, Robbie. This is one of those ultra rare books a paleographer only dreams of one day touching."

"Really?" Robbie truly was taken aback, not realizing the intrinsic value of a book he'd grown up with and had simply relegated to being more than their family Bible, more than "just another" of the many books his family had acquired over the generations. But if Father Dominic was so moved by it, perhaps he should reconsider his own relationship to it.

"To be honest, I haven't so much as even turned a page since I was a child. I'm sure no one here has. We just rather let it be."

"May I?" Michael asked, glancing at Robbie with an earnest and eager look.

"Yes, of course, absolutely. It's good this old thing will get some appreciation."

"Hana, take a look at this," Michael invited her. She and Aaron had still been gazing with admiration at the globe but she turned to join Michael. "This is one of those once-in-a-lifetime experiences, regardless of whether you're into bibles or not." He glanced down at her, smiling.

The priest began turning pages, taking in the beautiful calligraphy and large illustrated letters of the ancient scribes who had assembled this version, three columns per page. Typical of the era's style, there was no space between words; letters were all simply strung together, leaving it to the reader to parse the context and separate the word strings.

"Like the Codex Vaticanus, several passages of various gospels and books are missing. Let's take a look at Ecclesiastes. I've often found the tone of it melancholic or skeptical, since it raises questions about the meaning and purpose of human existence. I suppose that tone makes sense considering it is a series of meditations on the nature of life, the pursuit of knowledge and wisdom, and the inevitability of death."

He gently grabbed a thick handful of vellum pages, estimating the location, and carefully laid them on the left side of the easel. Coming up in the Book of Proverbs, he turned pages individually now, knowing he was close, since Ecclesiastes followed Proverbs in sequential order.

Each fine page of vellum turned with the sound of a satisfying crackle, the audible protest of stretched animal skin, something Michael always found soothing when working with ancient texts like this one. As he turned each page, he glanced at the workmanship, lost in the wonder of his quest.

Turning the next page, though, he noticed a small, loose piece of old parchment held flat against the book's spine gutter. It had clearly been there for some time, perhaps even centuries. He reached for it, gently coaxing it away from the vellum, to which it had nearly adhered itself over the ages.

"What's that?" Hana asked.

"I'm not sure. But let's find out, shall we?"

CHAPTER
THREE

Michael managed to pull the slip of parchment away from the vellum without damaging either page, then lifted it away from the codex. Despite its apparent age, the yellowed parchment was thin but durable, and in exceptionally good condition, measuring roughly six by nine inches.

As he moved to the window to better read it, Hana followed him out of curiosity. On the parchment were three stanzas of carefully prepared calligraphy in what appeared to Hana as some form of ancient language. Knowing Michael spoke several languages, old and modern, she turned to him.

"What language is that, Michael? I've never seen it before."

"Fascinating. It's Old English," Michael said, "the Anglo-Saxon language of the Middle Ages. And this looks to be the West Saxon dialect in some form of poetic verse. If memory serves, it would translate as something like:

"'In Sherborne chapel where the lady stands,
A hidden book awaits your hands.
Seek the truth by her eternal gaze,
Inscribed in stone through time's long maze.

Four virtues guard her, each a key,
Carved in stone for eternity
To find the order, think in pairs,
The holiest bond, the union that shares.

Unlock the virtues, left to right,
To reveal the path that's out of sight.
With two as one, and faith your guide,
Find Pontiff Johanna who lies inside.'

"Well, now. This *is* fascinating. Sherborne Abbey is somewhere around here in Wessex, isn't it, Robbie? As I recall, it was originally founded as a Saxon cathedral in the tenth century, and later converted into a Benedictine abbey."

"Did I hear you say Sherborne Abbey?" Robbie asked from across the room. He was showing Aaron the antique globe when he heard Michael mention it. "That's actually not far from here. What have you got there, Michael?"

"It's a small sheet of very old parchment I found lain against the spine of your Codex. It's actually quite intriguing, an ancient riddle of sorts. And of course I'm inclined to give it some thought, try to figure it out. Fortunately, I have one of the world's great puzzle solvers here with me." He grinned and nodded toward Hana, who blushed slightly.

Robbie crossed the room and was now looking over

Michael's shoulder. "That's odd," he observed. "I've never seen that before. You say it was tucked inside the pages?"

"Yes, between the end of the Book of Proverbs and the first page of Ecclesiastes, not that that's significant. At least I don't think it is." He sat down in one of two plush, overstuffed leather chairs beneath one of the windows. Hana perched next to him on the broad arm of the chair. Michael took out his notebook and wrote down the translation he'd rendered verbally.

"Now that is intriguing!" Hana said, engaging her inner puzzler. "But *'Johanna'*? Isn't that a woman's name?"

"*'Find Pontiff Johanna who lies inside'*... hmm." Michael turned slightly and stared out the window, taking in the soft, undulating hills of green as his mind worked the riddle.

"There is an old myth about an alleged female pope named Johanna, or Joan, in the ninth century which has always intrigued me. The legend claims she had dressed as a man all her life in order to better educate herself in the patriarchal, male-dominated culture of that era. And she supposedly assumed the regnal name of Pope John VIII."

"I like her already," Hana said, "but I've never heard of this legend of a female pope, though I must say it's about time—no offense to your Holy Father. But I simply can't imagine a woman would have been elected pope in the early Middle Ages, though I wish it were true. It was known as the Dark Ages, after all."

"No, you're right. But there's something else here that's piqued my interest. *'A hidden book awaits your hands...'* If it hasn't been discovered yet, wouldn't that be a fantastic find? And who knows what it might contain. And there *is* some documentation supporting Pope Joan's legitimacy that emerged a couple centuries after her supposed reign. On the whole, though, I'm dubious about the story—but this is just the kind of quest we love chasing down, isn't it?" He looked at Hana, mischief and a sense of adventure in his eyes.

"Hey, Robbie... feel like a little jaunt to Sherborne this afternoon?"

ROBBIE'S LAND Rover made good time to Sherborne Abbey, some forty-five minutes from Saxon Hall in one of Britain's most picturesque towns. Sherborne was a charming and typically English market town, brimming with history and heritage, its honey-colored hamstone buildings glowing brightly under the afternoon sun. Adjacent to the abbey was Sherborne Castle, a 16th-century mansion built by Sir Walter Raleigh, one of the most prominent figures of the Elizabethan era.

The stone walls surrounding the abbey rose next to a field of chestnut trees along a flowing stream that ran through the town, branching from the River Yeo. The abbey itself was built in the shape of a cross, with a bell tower marking its apex. The stone work was impeccable, with overgrown ivy arching the entrance, graceful spires rising into the sky, glimmering ivory towers and elegant arched cloisters. The Gothic architecture was a perfect balance of delicate ornamentation and inspired grandeur. The sun caught the stonework in brilliant flashes and the leaded glass windows illuminated the abbey with a warm, golden light.

A smell of incense lingered in the air, along with a wafting scent of amber resin, citrus and sagebrush, muted by damp earth fused with moss that grew on the abbey walls, and drifting fireplace soot from a nearby village.

"This place is just magical," Hana sighed dreamily, taking in the tranquil scents and architectural delights as the four of them ambled toward the abbey's arched entryway.

"It is kind of a lazy day," Aaron added, "made more so by this place. What is it about ancient abbeys that makes one feel so... I don't know... as familiar as the comforting touch of an old, time-worn book?"

"Well," Michael began, sensing his cue, "apart from the historic architectural and aesthetic beauty—you know, visually captivating features like stained glass windows, paintings, frescoes and sculptures—there's a sense of history and tradition... a connection to nature and the divine, helping people feel more connected to something greater than themselves. And, of course, there's a quiet and stillness here, with a focus on meditation, prayer and reflection. These are all soothing and restorative qualities, helping people feel more calm and centered in a world filled largely with gloom and doom in the news."

Aaron looked at him sidelong, as if appraising him anew. "Well said, Michael. I couldn't have put it better myself. Your words give me a sense of peace."

"Just doing my job," the priest said, winking at his friend.

Stepping inside the abbey, the first thing to strike everyone was the vaulted ceiling, adorned with intricate fan tracery creating a delicate and ethereal atmosphere.

The tall, slender windows allowed streams of light to fill the chapel, illuminating the ancient stonework and enhancing the sense of sacredness within.

The second thing was the angry figure approaching them in a rush—a tall, thin man with a hawkish beak of a nose, wearing a tweed coat and black fedora, with a churlish countenance in stark contrast to the otherwise serene setting of this ancient place of worship.

"Get out of my way!" the man grumbled as he rudely brushed them aside with a wave of his cane on his way out the door, which he intentionally slammed behind him. The harsh closure echoed off the stone walls of the abbey, dampening the still sense of tranquility felt by its new arrivals.

Then they noticed the vicar standing in the shadows, looking timid and chastened.

"I regret you had to witness that spectacle. Please accept my sincere apologies," he said in a hushed tone, his timorous voice bearing a raspy, almost hoarse quality to it, muted as if speaking through a veil. It was a voice that betrayed a touch of melancholy or world-weariness to the man's words, as if he'd used them many times under similar circumstances. Noticing Michael's white collar notch, his tone changed a bit.

"Ah, welcome to Sherborne Abbey, Father. I am the vicar here, Reverend Warren Andrews, at your service. Please, make yourselves comfortable. I'll be up in my office should you have any questions about the Abbey." He then receded back into the shadows and quietly ascended a flight of stairs to the floor above.

"What do you suppose *that* was all about?" Hana asked no one in particular. "Who was that awful man?"

"Well, he was one troubled soul, that much was

clear," Michael said. "He must have had words with Reverend Andrews, I imagine. But don't let him spoil the atmosphere. Let's enjoy this beautiful sanctuary."

In the narthex, just inside the entrance, Hana found a small wooden rack of brochures describing the abbey. She picked one up and started reading.

As he usually did when entering a place of worship new to him, Michael took in every detail: the many stained glass windows; the intersecting wings of the transept, typical of Gothic architecture; the choir stalls topped by a decorative canopy called a baldachin; and —as Victoria had insisted they not miss—the Lady Chapel, a smaller chapel at the eastern end of the north transept characterized by its ornate decoration and beautiful stained glass windows. Its walls were adorned with intricate stone carvings, including a series of niches that contained statues of various saints. The high vaulted ceiling was decorated with painted motifs, including a depiction of the Assumption of Mary into heaven.

The Lady Chapel's main feature was its stunning east window, which dated back to the early sixteenth century. Divided into panels that depicted scenes from the life of Mary, as well as various biblical figures and saints, the colors and details of the window were breathtaking, with a wide range of hues and intricate traits that created a sense of depth and movement.

One of the most striking features of the chapel was the tomb of Sir John Horsey and his wife Lady Margaret, which was located in a recess in the south wall. The tomb was made from alabaster and featured intricate carvings and an effigy of the couple lying side by side, their stone hands clasped in prayer. Hana and Michael walked into that area while Aaron and Robbie remained in the main chapel admiring the stained glass windows.

Still holding the brochure, Hana read from it: "*Sir John Horsey was one of Henry VIII's most loyal knights, and was a prominent figure here in Dorset, serving as high sheriff in 1537 and knight of the shire in 1539.*"

"That's quite the honor he and his wife were given. This is an impressive tomb, especially given its life-size effigies," Michael noted.

The altar in the Lady Chapel was simple but elegant, made from locally quarried Purbeck marble believed to date back to the twelfth century. In a small arched alcove on the wall behind the altar was an ancient, half-meter high statue of the Virgin Mary, to whom the chapel was dedicated, its visage among the most moving Michael had ever beheld. It was as if her eyes followed him wherever he moved.

Hypnotized by the image, Michael whispered, "'*In Sherborne chapel where the lady stands…*' Hana, come look at this!"

Hana moved next to him and followed his gaze to the statue.

"I see what you mean. It's a startling image, isn't it? I'm guessing this is '*where the lady stands*'?"

He looked around to be certain the rector remained downstairs. "I wish Karl were here. He's so much better at skullduggery than I am. Pity he's on vacation."

"What are you planning to do, Father Dominic?" Hana asked tauntingly.

"Why, simply take a closer look. I mean, that verse is centuries old and could have meant nothing. Even if it had, surely anything secreted here would have long since been discovered, right?"

He raised an eyebrow to Hana as if seeking permission, and she just shook her head with a smile. They'd found the most amazing things in times past by simply looking.

Michael ascended the two steps to the altar, then moved around it to the arched alcove against the back wall featuring the Madonna that had so captivated him. Glancing behind him again, he motioned for Hana to keep guard for anyone entering the chapel's transept. It would be embarrassing for a priest to be caught tampering with such a prominent shrine.

Inspecting the small statuette, he tried lifting it, but it felt loosely fastened to its base, which on its own seemed unmovable. Then he noticed there were four words engraved horizontally on the stones in the wall behind the Madonna. Each word appeared on its own stone brick. Michael read them aloud. *"Humility. Purity. Obedience. Piety.* Those words are etched into the stone here, Hana, obviously symbolizing Mary's virtues." Noticing the grout between each brick didn't look to be fully sealed, he reached out to touch one. It moved slightly under his pressure. He reached over to touch the next brick, and the other two after that. Each of them wobbled a bit.

"This is strange. Each of these words are on singular stone bricks, and each brick feels a little loose." He tried prying one out of its placement—to see if there was anything hidden behind it—but it resisted the attempt, seemingly locked in place. Then he tried gently pushing on one. It gave in ever so slightly, perhaps half an inch.

Michael's excitement mounted as he realized he might be on to something, when suddenly a stern voice from behind him broke the silence.

"You're obviously looking for something, Father. Would you care to tell me what it is?"

Surprised, Michael whipped around.

The cranky old man in the fedora was standing there in the shadows, his black cane waving in the air, pointing at Michael.

CHAPTER

FOUR

S tartled by the man's sudden appearance, Michael glanced at Hana, who shrugged with eyes wide open, as if she too were surprised the man had apparently materialized out of thin air.

"Who might you be, if I may ask?" Michael ventured.

"No, you may *not*," the old curmudgeon said flatly. His accent was distinctly Received Pronunciation, signaling he was likely of the British upper class. "If you're done messing about back there, I suggest you return to the ambulatory here. I take it you are Father Dominic? From the Vatican?"

Michael was stunned. How could anyone here in England *possibly* know who he was?!

"I'd be more inclined to answer if I knew who was asking," he replied, masking his surprise.

The man looked thoughtful as he leaned forward on his cane, on the handle of which was the chrome body of a pouncing jaguar. He softened his tone, though there was still an authoritative edge to it.

"My name is Pelham. *Lord* Lucius Pelham. This abbey —in fact the entire town of Sherborne—has been on my family's land for centuries. And while the abbey is Church of England, like yourself I happen to be Roman Catholic. What brings you here, Father?"

"We were, uh, just admiring the Lady Chapel, Lord Pelham, and in particular that remarkable statue of the Madonna." Michael decided not to offer more than was necessary at the moment, cautiously deferential to this mercurial stranger.

"I meant, what brings you to Sherborne? It's rather out of the way for a man in your position."

Disturbed that this man clearly knew more about Michael than he knew about the man, the priest returned to the ambulatory and stood within feet of the stranger.

"We're just visiting friends at Saxon Hall for a few days, while taking in the sights," Michael said, holding Pelham's gaze as he spoke.

Pelham considered this for a time, looking long and hard into Michael's eyes. Then he spoke, very slowly. "Ah, yes. I see… staying with Clan Anglicus now, are you?" He seemed to give this further reflection, as if he wasn't pleased but there was nothing he could do about it.

"Well, carry on then. Just take care to mind your business in this sacred space." Turning, he hobbled toward the north vestry of the chapel, the tap of his cane echoing in the airy chamber. He opened what now appeared to be a hidden door in the wall adorned with carvings of vines and flowers, then vanished.

"Well, that would explain why I didn't see him come in," Hana said after Pelham had gone. "Why would there be a secret door in an abbey? And how do you suppose he knew your name?"

As Michael shrugged, Robbie stepped forward from the main chapel, Aaron close behind him. "I'd wager a guess that would be the handiwork of our Miss Charlotte, Saxon Hall's head housekeeper and relentless town gossip. She was told you'd be coming."

"Well, I do admit to being shocked when Lord Pelham spoke my name, and he seemed to know a good deal about me, meaning he's taken the time to do his research," Michael said. "But yes, that would make sense. Word seems to travel fast in small towns like this, I guess. And I suppose he was justified a bit to address us."

Michael looked sheepishly at Hana, who shrugged. He then explained briefly to the other two about finding the four words carved in bricks behind the statue of the Virgin Mary and their assumption this was from the clue they'd discovered in the Bible. Aaron and Robbie both lit up at the possibilities.

"Then back to the task at hand," Aaron prompted, eager to continue their search, "maybe the '*Lady*' in the riddle doesn't refer to the Virgin Mary at all, but to Lady Margaret Horsey, who's entombed with her husband, Sir John, beneath their joined effigies."

"Good point," Michael acknowledged, "I hadn't thought of that. And both *are* here in the 'Lady' Chapel." He moved over to the Horsey tomb and bent down to examine the top and base of the sarcophagus, running his hands along the raised effigies. "Well, this appears to be completely sealed. If there are secret compartments, they're sure well hidden." Just then Michael heard some movement in the entry to the chapel and knew there would be no ability to re-examine that loose brick, or anything else for the moment.

"Let's get back to Saxon Hall and give this more thought. Now that we have a better idea of what the abbey looks like, things may make more sense after analyzing the riddle a bit more. And I'd like to ask Victoria what she knows about this peculiar Lord Pelham."

"AH, so you've already met our irascible lord of the realm, have you?" Victoria replied when Michael asked her about his new acquaintance. "He's a character, that one. Thinks he owns the town, he does. But be careful with him, Father. There's something off about His Lordship. It's a small town, you see, and word has it that he has deep connections in the Vatican. I seem to recall he belongs to some mysterious organization that goes back centuries... what was that name? Ah, yes: the Order of Papal Guardians, that's it. I remember the acronym OPG because townsfolk here called them 'Old Pompous Geezers!' I have no idea what their mission is, or if they even have one. But that's really all I know, apart from him being a thorn in the side of most everyone in town."

"The Order of Papal Guardians? I've never heard of them," Michael said. "But I will do some research, since it does sound like something I should know about, especially if their objective deals at all with being 'papal guardians.' Thank you, Victoria, I knew you were the person to ask."

"Not at all, a pleasure to oblige. Just steer clear of him, as I said. He's a mischief-maker, that one."

. . .

RETURNING TO THE LIBRARY, Michael and Hana each took a copy of the translation he had worked out earlier and—sitting by the window as the sun began to set, each of them in one of the two leather armchairs—they began deconstructing the ancient riddle:

In Sherborne chapel where the lady stands,
A hidden book awaits your hands.
Seek the truth by her eternal gaze,
Inscribed in stone through time's long maze.

Four virtues guard her, each a key,
Carved in stone for eternity:
To find the order, think in pairs,
The holiest bond, the union that shares.

Unlock the virtues, left to right,
To reveal the path that's out of sight.
With two as one, and faith your guide,
Find Pontiff Johanna who lies inside.

Since the first two lines were clear enough, Hana began with the third line of the first stanza. "'*Seek the truth by her eternal gaze*' must refer to that statue of the Madonna, and what you discovered with that Mona Lisa effect it possessed, where her eyes appeared to follow you as you moved around the chapel. And there's a '*truth*' connected to that somehow, one that's '*inscribed in stone.*' That must refer to the four words you found! What were they again?"

"Humility, Purity, Obedience, and Piety."

"So, '*to find the order, think in pairs*' must obviously mean there's a specific order to the words."

"Oh, wait," Michael interjected. "Since we were surprised by Lord Pelham's sudden appearance, I forgot to mention that each stone containing a word appears to be movable! I only had time to press in on one and it gives in slightly. Maybe that's what this means, that there's some order or combination of the words in pairs that '*unlocks the virtues, left to right!*' But what does it unlock, I wonder? It's got to be the '*hidden book*' that '*awaits our hands,*' wouldn't you think?"

Hana was now fully engaged, her enthusiasm reflected in the accelerated pace of her speech. "'*The holiest bond, the union that shares*' would confirm what you just said, yes! The holiest bond could refer to marriage— perhaps meaning marrying the pairs of words? If so, I figure there are many permutations for rearranging the four words in various orders, but only twelve for pairing them up, including reverse order, as in:

"Humility-Purity
Humility-Obedience
Humility-Piety
Purity-Humility
Purity-Obedience
Purity-Piety
Obedience-Humility
Obedience-Purity
Obedience-Piety
Piety-Humility
Piety-Obedience
Piety-Purity"

"But then, of course, we'd have to add in the second pair, in which the various four-word combinations might seem endless. But we've got time," Hana added, smiling confidently. "We'll just take it on patiently."

"What would I do without you?" Michael said, looking at her fondly. "That's brilliant. So we just need to try pressing the stones in up to, what, twenty-four different orders until—well, I don't know what happens then. But we'll find out!

"Now," he continued, "what about, *'With two as one, and faith your guide?'* I think we've got the faith part well in hand, but *'with two as one?'* Good grief, Hana. While we're both drawn to puzzles, you have far more patience than I do in solving them. What's the attraction?"

Hana smiled as if comforting a child. "Puzzles stimulate the brain and provide an intellectual challenge for me, Michael, which I find engaging and satisfying. They require critical thinking, problem-solving, pattern recognition, and logical reasoning skills, all of which are both enjoyable and rewarding, while providing a sense of achievement and satisfaction like few other things do, for me anyway. On the face of it, this one seems fairly straightforward. But, remember that keystone puzzle we were challenged by at Rosslyn Chapel in Scotland? Now *that* was a tough one, and yet, we ultimately figured it out."

"You're right, of course. We are an invincible team, aren't we?" Michael looked at Hana again, this time with something more in his contemplation of her. Recognizing the limitations of their relationship, he felt a sudden sense of melancholy about the situation, briefly mourning the potential for a romantic connection and the sacrifices he had made in choosing his religious path. Looking down at his notebook, he quietly sighed.

"Are you alright, Michael? You suddenly went somewhere else."

He looked up quickly, feigning a smile and chipper attitude he didn't feel in the least. "Sure, I'm fine. Just focused on solving this riddle...

"Say," he brightened, changing the subject, "why don't we call Karl and Lukas and invite them to join us? I expect their itinerary is fairly loose, at least that's what Karl implied when they took off for Paris. And I'm sure they'll enjoy being part of this hunt of ours. Worth a try, anyway."

"That's a great idea," Hana said. "The boys will love this." As she watched him take out his phone to call Karl, she sensed his sorrow, though she could only guess as to what might have caused it. But she had a pretty good idea what it was... the unspoken plight they both shared. She respected his commitment to his calling as a priest but could still mourn—as she sensed he did—for the relationship they could share if only he had chosen a different path.

ON THE SECOND-FLOOR platform of the Eiffel Tower, Karl Dengler and Lukas Bischoff were standing outside by the guardrail—a protective barrier that runs along the perimeter of the platform—taking in the sunset over Paris at the end of their first week on holiday from their Swiss Guard duties in the Vatican. As the sun began to dip below the horizon, the sky transformed into a stunning array of colors, ranging from bright oranges and pinks to deep purples and blues. The clouds took on a mellow, golden hue, and the light shimmered off the surface of the Seine River as it wound its way through the city below them.

Karl threw his arm around Lukas in a warm embrace. "Wouldn't it be great if we could just sleep right here overnight? I couldn't think of a more romantic place for camping out."

"Well, it doesn't give us much privacy," Lukas pointed out, "and there's no room service." They both laughed.

"Speaking of food," Karl added, "I'm starving. Let's go find a quaint bistro for dinner. I've got a craving for French onion soup and a fresh baguette."

"My mouth is watering already. Lead on."

As they headed toward the elevator, Karl's cell phone vibrated in his pocket. Removing it, he saw it was Michael calling. He put it on speaker so Lukas could hear.

"Hey, Father Michael! You wouldn't believe where we are at this very moment."

There was a pause, then Michael ventured, "At the top of the Eiffel Tower?"

"Close enough!" Karl said, laughing. "How could you possibly have known that?!"

"It wasn't a stretch to guess that one, Karl. The two of you, in Paris at sunset? Your voice pretty much alluded to it anyway. So listen… do you guys have firm plans for the next few days?"

"Well, we were thinking of going either to Amsterdam or London for our second week, but we're flexible. Did you have something in mind?" Karl knew

Michael well enough to know he wouldn't ask such a leading question without some purpose.

"Hana, Aaron and I are with Robbie Anglicus, a friend of Aaron's, not far from a little English town called Sherborne. We'd love to have you join us, and as usual, there may be some excitement in store for you. For all of us, actually. I can explain more when we see you. So… will we see you?" he prodded.

Lukas nodded enthusiastically. "You bet!" Karl affirmed. "We'll head to Calais in the morning and take the Channel Tunnel, so we should see you by late afternoon. How will we find you?"

"Just set your GPS for Sherborne Abbey. Text me when you're an hour out and we'll meet you there. Accommodations are already set for you here at Robbie's house so no worries there."

"Looking forward to it, Michael. See you then."

FIVE

"We'll revisit the Abbey when Karl and Lukas arrive," Michael said to Hana. "I suppose we'll find out what that '*two as one*' means when we get there. Or, maybe not. But I am convinced those stones are involved, somehow. I'm really curious to see if our word-pairing theory works and what happens when the bricks are pressed. Can you imagine? Whatever it turns out to be, we're probably the first people in centuries to have discovered this!"

"Not so fast, my friend. This whole thing may turn out to be nothing more than a wild goose chase."

"Lord, I hope not. It's not often one chances upon such seductive historical treasures like this. It's *got* to lead us somewhere."

As Karl's Jeep Wrangler pulled up to Sherborne Abbey, the late afternoon sun was starting to set, and the scene was a glorious welcome for both Karl and Lukas. The abbey's stone walls and towers were bathed in a summery, golden light. The west front of the building was particularly impressive, with a magnificent array of carved stone figures and intricate decoration. The large west window, dating back to the fifteenth century, caught the last rays of the sun and glowed brightly in the fading light.

As the boys were taking it all in, a white Land Rover pulled up next to the Wrangler. Michael, Hana, Aaron and Robbie all got out and greeted their friends with smiles and hugs, with Michael introducing them to Robbie.

"Isn't this a fantastic place?" Michael enthused to the new arrivals, pointing out its features. "The exterior of the abbey is a beautiful mix of Norman and Gothic styles, with some parts of the building dating back to the eighth century. And over there on the south side of the abbey is the stunning Golden Porch, adorned with intricate carvings and easily one of the finest examples of medieval stone carving in all of England. It's one of the most beautiful places I've seen in a long while. Plus, we've got a potential mystery waiting for us inside."

"A mystery?" Karl asked, grinning at Lukas. "Tell us more!"

Michael filled them in on the parchment he found in the Codex Anglicus, the history he knew of the alleged Pope Joan, and the stones he discovered when examining the alcove just behind the Madonna statue.

"Well, what are we waiting for?" Karl exclaimed. "Let's see what's inside!"

Hana watched Michael interacting with the boys. He had that look in his eyes. The kind he always got when anticipating a new discovery of ancient history and sharing it with others. She was so happy for him but hoped that whatever awaited them panned out. She didn't want him to be disappointed.

THE ABBEY WAS empty of people when they entered, the only sign of recent presence being the flickering of votive candles lining the north and south aisles. Six pairs of footsteps echoed throughout the lofty space as they wordlessly made their way to the abbey's far eastern alcove where the Lady Chapel was nestled.

As Michael expected, Karl and Lukas showed due respect for the beauty of the abbey itself, and the Lady Chapel in particular. Since both of them knew every nook and cranny of the Vatican, and St. Peter's Basilica in particular, their instincts were seasoned as to the makeup of sacred spaces. And while there was no comparison in scale to the two, the Lady Chapel had more than enough sanctified spiritual space to move both young men to awe, especially given its age and place in history.

"So, take us through this riddle you mentioned, Father Michael," Lukas said. "Perhaps it will allow us to help you better."

Michael removed the translation from his pocket and handed it to Lukas. Karl looked over his shoulder as they both read it together.

"And you found this in the Codex Anglicus, you said?" Karl asked. "I wonder how such a thing ended up at Saxon Hall in the first place... I mean, where is the connection, I wonder? Is the Anglicus family somehow related to Sherborne Abbey?"

Everyone looked at Robbie, who suddenly blushed.

"Well, I certainly can't explain it! I had no idea of that parchment being in our Bible. I still find it strange that no one had discovered it in all these years. But as I said, we rarely ever need to actually use it. The book just sits there in the library, as I'm sure it has for generations."

"Michael," Hana began, rereading the riddle as she stood next to Karl, "looking at this again, I'm sure you're right: *'Four virtues guard her, each a key, carved in stone for eternity. To find the order, think in pairs...'* That would surely lead us to the four stones, the words of virtue carved into each one, and pairing the words up in some suitable combination. So, we just need to find the right 'marriage,' the *'holiest bond,'* though I don't quite understand *'the union that shares'* bit. One piece at a time, though."

Michael moved back behind the altar again, positioning himself in front of the half-meter-high statue of the Madonna with the four horizontal bricks behind her in the alcove.

"Okay. What would you start with, then?" he asked Hana.

"Let's go from the top and work our way down in double pairs. So first would be *'Humility-Purity-Obedience-Piety.'*"

Michael looked at the four stones each with the carved virtue on it, the given order in the alcove wall being the same as the first combination Hana gave him: *Humility, Purity, Obedience,* and *Piety*. Pressing the stones in sequential order, each brick receded a half inch, then popped back out as each subsequent brick was pressed.

"They're definitely connected!" Michael exulted. "There must be some ancient mechanism each stone is coupled with. Amazing. Okay, what's next?"

"'*Humility-Piety-Obedience-Purity*.'" Hana had worked up her own logical formula for reading off the various permutations to Michael, checking off each combination after giving it to him.

After another dozen or so attempts with nothing more happening, Michael began questioning the sanity of his actions and whether his suspicions were justified, when suddenly—after pressing in the fourth stone for the combination *Obedience-Purity-Humility-Piety*—a loud click was heard coming from somewhere behind them.

Michael looked at the others. "Did you hear that?" Everyone nodded silently, all heads already turned, searching for the sound's location. "Any idea where it came from?"

Karl walked over to the Horsey sarcophagus. "I could swear it was in this area, Michael. Can you make it happen again?"

"Let me try." The priest again pressed the stones in, repeating the pattern—*Obedience-Purity-Humility-Piety*—and again, a loud click was heard. It was definitely coming from the Horsey tomb, where Karl was now standing.

"It's here, for sure," he said, kneeling down behind the alabaster heads of the effigies and looking at them more closely. "That sound seems to be coming from Lady Margaret's head. Wait a minute... what's this?"

Karl noticed something he hadn't seen before—a small metal shaft about an inch long had popped out from under the base of the sarcophagus, parallel to the floor. "It looks to be some kind of lever, Michael." Reaching down, he tried moving it—from side to side, in and out—but it wouldn't budge.

"It doesn't seem to do anything..."

Michael, who had been standing in front of the Madonna statue as all this was taking place, suddenly noticed the sculpture had turned slightly. It was not facing straight ahead as it was before.

"Okay, this is a little creepy. I swear this statue moved, though I didn't see it happen while I was watching Karl. But it's definitely turned now from where it was facing before. There *must* be a connection."

Hana thought a moment, her head leaning to one side as she considered something.

"Wait. Remember the riddle said, '*With two as one, and faith your guide*?' Maybe it takes two of us doing something at the same time to make this whole thing work." Moving to where Michael was, she inspected the statue more closely now, feeling for any potential movement as she grasped it with her hands. "Yes, it does seem to be less fixed now! I'm pretty sure it can turn. Karl, try to flip that lever as I turn this."

Karl got down on both knees, bent over, and put all his strength into grasping the tiny lever with his thumb and forefinger, trying to make it move one way or the other. As Hana turned the Madonna clockwise, with Karl's thumb burning from the pressure, the lever eventually began to move as Hana continued to turn the statue.

"They *do* move together!" she rejoiced, thrilled her puzzling skills again proved useful.

And as the lever went from its original position to the opposite side, a hidden drawer suddenly popped open beneath Lady Margaret's head, adjacent to where the lever was.

"Here it is!" Karl said. "A drawer just opened." Everyone moved to where Karl was kneeling, anxious to see what was to be found. Just the front edge of a drawer had opened, inviting someone to pull it out fully. All six pairs of eyes fixed on the small opening.

"Then that would confirm the married Horsey couple's role as being '*the union that shares*' part of the riddle," Hana said.

Smiling in victory, Karl looked up at the priest. "Michael, would you like to do the honors?"

CHAPTER
SIX

As the others moved back a little, Michael knelt by the effigy of Lady Margaret. He reached down to pull out the narrow drawer, which creaked open with a rusty groan. The priest's trembling hands fumbled in the dim light as the drawer clicked against its backstop, revealing its contents.

Inside was a small book, roughly eight inches long, its yellowed vellum pages perhaps an inch deep, with thick boards front and back featuring intricately carved ivory embellishments and the embossed image of a coat of arms on the cover. Michael gently removed it from the drawer.

As he held the book in his hands, he couldn't believe his luck. He had stumbled upon a rare and valuable piece of hidden history. The coat of arms on the cover caught his eye, and he wondered whose it was and what the images in each embellishment symbolized. As he opened the book, he realized it was a diary, written in a delicate and flowing script in the ancient Anglo-Saxon language. The entries were dated in the mid 800s, and Michael felt a sense of awe and wonder as he scanned the words of its long-dead author.

But who was *the author?* he wondered.

Turning to the first few pages, he read aloud the inscription on the first written page, slowly translating from the Old English as he made out each word: *"I declare this to be my confidential journal for the eyes of no other but history,"* and below that, in the same beautiful script, was the shocking identity of its author: *"Holy Mother Pope Johanna Anglicus as John VIII."*

Slack-jawed, Michael looked up at the others, his brows raised in amazement.

"It's true, then... There *was* a female pope named Johanna, or Joan!" he exclaimed.

"And she holds my family's surname—*Anglicus!*" Robbie said excitedly. "So we *must* be related. I'm just gobsmacked by this whole thing!"

"What else does she say?" Hana asked, her hand anxiously touching Michael's sleeve, prompting him to proceed. "Open to a random page and read it."

Michael did as she asked, flipping through to the first full page of the diary and translating the opening entry as he read it to the others:

"12th March 856, Rome —

Verily, as a woman who finds herself enrobed in the mantle of leadership within the Catholic Church, I am in a constant dance upon a precarious tightrope. On the one hand, I take pride in my womanhood, for it bestows upon me a unique lens through which to view my sacred duties. Yet, on the other hand, I am well aware that the male-dominated hierarchy of the Church would never extend their embrace if they were privy to the truth of my gender.

Each passing day reminds me of the immense challenges that befall me as a woman traversing a world crafted by men. I remain ever vigilant, scrutinizing my every step, meticulously selecting my words so as not to expose my true identity. I must tread with caution, lest I be perceived as too tender or excessively emotional, as such qualities may be deemed vulnerabilities. Simultaneously, I dare not exert too much force or exhibit excessive assertiveness, for fear of transgressing the boundaries imposed upon me.

Living in this perpetual state of watchfulness is profoundly draining, for I am forever tormented by the fear of discovery. Nevertheless, I comprehend the magnitude of the risks at hand and cannot afford to lower my guard. Were the truth to be unveiled, not only would it spell the end of my papacy but perchance even the termination of my very existence.

Yet, despite the manifold tribulations, I am imbued with a profound sense of purpose and contentment within my role as Pope. I understand that I answer to a divine summons, and my leadership manifests a tangible impact upon the lives of countless faithful Catholics across the world.

Ultimately, my essence transcends the boundaries imposed by my gender, and it does not confine the scope of my accomplishments. As Pope, I stand resolved to continue guiding with unwavering courage, unyielding conviction, and a profound faith in the omnipotence of God's love to vanquish all hindrances."

"Do you have any idea what this means?!" the priest marveled as he folded the book upon his chest. "It would be history-changing, even mind-altering for the Church and the faithful it serves. That is, if this is in fact an authentic creation of Joan herself *as pope*, and not some impostor. Though this goes against my natural skepticism of such things, for now let's assume this *is* the work of history's only female pontiff, and listen to what she has to say. There may be so much to learn here. We can work on the authentication when we return to Rome— assuming we are permitted to take this. I'll have to speak with Reverend Andrews. But I'd like more to go on, more surety of what we have before speaking with him."

"I agree," Hana spoke up. "I hear the pure, compassionate voice of a determined woman in those words. One who clearly took her historic role seriously. As you say, Michael, I think '*for now*' to assume this is authentic is a safe assumption." She glanced around the chapel. "Why don't we put everything back the way it was and return to Saxon Hall to give this diary a more fitting read?"

"We're on it," Karl said, as he and Lukas moved to reset the drawer, statue and stones, hiding any signs there had been a discovery made in the chapel. Giving the space a last once-over, Michael led them out of the abbey and back to their cars.

ONCE EVERYONE HAD LEFT the building, Reverend Warren Andrews, the diffident vicar of Sherborne Abbey, emerged from the Lady Chapel's second floor gallery, where he had been hiding in the shadows while overhearing everything as events unfolded below him.

Not one to provoke a confrontation—even in his own domain—Andrews watched and listened as the priest and his friends worked out some riddle on a notepad, then spent some time manipulating the stonework behind the Madonna—bricks even the vicar himself hadn't known were movable. But he had found other secrets in the abbey over the years, so he wasn't surprised.

If what they found was true, the shock of their finding the diary of this so-called *female* Pope Joan was completely unexpected, and undoubtedly an earth-shattering discovery.

And he was certain his master would want to know.

CHAPTER
SEVEN

B ack in the library at Saxon Hall and now alone, Michael—as he was usually inclined to do with new artifacts he discovered in the field—took out his phone and snapped photographs of every page in the small book, in case anything were to happen to it or, in this case, if Reverend Andrews decided not to let him take it back to the Vatican, which was a long shot anyway.

As he flipped through to the last page, Michael suddenly spied a small, ancient coin mounted to the back cover board. Carefully removing it, his heart pounding with excitement, he realized what he was now holding was a rare exemplar of papal monogram coinage. He could only hope it was attributed to Pope Joan.

He carefully inspected the medallion, knowing that in the ninth century popes began issuing their own coins as a sign of their tremendous power and authority over Rome and its empire. These coins held a unique identifier—a combination of characters or symbols representing the name of the reigning pope at that time.

Papal coins typically featured a Latin monogram on their faces—in this case, SCS PETRVS, IOHANS, signifying Sanctus (Saint) Peter and [Pope] John (or Joan)—usually accompanied by a Christian cross to further emphasize the religious nature of it. The reverse side held an image of Saint Peter or similar religious symbol; on this coin, Michael noted the reverse identified Holy Roman Emperor Louis II, shown in Latin as "LVDOVVICUS IMP."

Hana, Aaron, Robbie, Karl and Lukas were chattering as a group when they entered the library, all having freshened up in their rooms before dinner.

"You won't believe what I found inside the back of the diary," the priest marveled as they gathered around him. "This could be part of the growing pool of evidence that Joan did in fact exist! There can be no other explanation."

Showing them the coin, he explained its purpose and history as the artifact was passed around the group, each person aware they were holding hidden history in their hands—possibly the first time in nearly twelve hundred years the coin had been handled.

Everyone took seats as Michael—from the comfort of his now favorite leather chair by the window—opened the diary and prepared to read the next entry for everyone.

Robbie had invited Victoria to join them, having told her of the newly-discovered parchment hidden within the pages of their family Bible and their exploits at the abbey. She had prepared a large, steaming pot of Earl Grey tea for everyone and, once cups had been prepared and passed around, Michael began reading.

"7th April 856, Rome —

I pen this entry in the deepest of secrecy, given the weight of my responsibilities and the burden of the hidden truth that lies upon my shoulders. As Pope, I have been entrusted with a sacred duty to lead the Church, its faithful flock, and guide them towards salvation, albeit while concealing my true feminine nature. Yet, there is a more powerful secret which has been passed down to me from my predecessors, a hidden truth that I discovered during my research in the Vatican Archives—a secret that could shake the very foundation of the Church and alter its course for generations to come.

The secret lies within an ancient, hidden manuscript, written in a language barely understood today. I have studied the text diligently, seeking the confidential guidance of scholars and theologians to decipher its meaning. The manuscript, it seems, is the lost Gospel of St. Salome, a disciple of Christ who was one of the first women to follow Jesus during his ministry on earth, and who had been erased from the annals of history for reasons unknown. Despite facing persecution and discrimination because of her gender, Salome remained steadfast in her faith and played a key role in spreading the message of Christ throughout Galilee and beyond.

The Gospel of St. Salome reveals a message different from the established teachings of the Church, a message that emphasizes the importance of love, compassion, and equality above all else. It tells of Christ's ministry in a new light, one where He championed the rights of the oppressed, fought against the corrupt authorities, and sought to build a community where all were equal in the eyes of God.

The Gospel speaks of Christ's message as one of unity and acceptance, transcending the boundaries of race, gender, and social status. It reveals that the early Church included both men and women as leaders.

As I read the Gospel, I felt a deep stirring within my soul. I recognized the profound wisdom in the words, the truth that had been obscured by the hands of time and the manipulations of those who sought to maintain power. The implications of this discovery are immense, as it challenges the very authority upon which the Church has been built.

Yet, I fear the consequences of revealing this secret to the world. I worry that it will divide the faithful, leading to discord and strife among the people. I worry about the wrath of those who will feel threatened by the truth and the potential for the Church to lose its influence in a world that desperately needs its guiding light.

As Pope, I am faced with a dilemma that will ultimately define my papacy. In my heart, I feel torn between the obligation to maintain the unity and stability of the Church and the desire to bring forth this transformative knowledge. I know that revealing this secret could lead to upheaval and division within the Church. It reveals that the role of women in the Church has been suppressed for centuries due to political and social pressures. It would mean challenging the long-held beliefs and doctrines that have shaped the faith for centuries. Yet, I cannot help but feel that, in a world riddled with conflict and division, the message of unity and acceptance found within this lost gospel could be the key to healing and moving the Church forward.

For now, I continue to carry this secret, praying for wisdom and discernment as I navigate the treacherous waters of my papal duties. May the Lord grant me the strength and courage to do what is right, for the sake of the Church and the salvation of all humanity."

The room was dead quiet when Michael finished reading, each person pondering Pope Joan's plight and the fate of the lost Gospel, when Victoria finally broke the silence.

"I must say, this is the story of an incredibly courageous woman, especially during an age when women were less than second-class citizens," she said earnestly. "I wish we had more women like her today in the clergy —especially in the Catholic Church." She glanced at Michael and gave him a knowing smile. It was a source of pride for their parishioners that the Church of England had begun ordination of female priests in 1994.

"As many of you may know," Michael offered, "tradition holds that Salome the Myrrh Bearer, also known as St. Salome of Jerusalem, was one of the women who witnessed the crucifixion of Jesus and went to his tomb on the third day to anoint his body. She is mentioned in the Gospels of Mark and Matthew as one of the women who, along with Mary Magdalene and others, witnessed the empty tomb."

"I wonder what became of that lost Gospel of St. Salome," Hana ventured. "It would be fascinating to read her personal views of Christ's mission from a first-hand observer."

"Like most documentation from that era, it's very likely long lost," Aaron said. "Though she did say she discovered it in the Secret Archives. Perhaps it's still there, buried somewhere deep. But yes, finding something like that would be a historic discovery of epic proportions."

"Actually," Michael spoke up as he'd continued reading the next entry, "Joan makes reference to it again here...

"12th May 856, Rome —

It has been some days since I last wrote about the Gospel of St. Salome, but recent events have compelled me to return to the subject. I have spent many sleepless nights reflecting on this hidden treasure, contemplating the fate of its teachings and the responsibility that lies with me.

I have come to learn that Salome's Gospel is not only obscured by the sands of time, but also intentionally hidden by a secretive organization called the Order of Papal Guardians. They have existed for centuries, their sole purpose being to protect the Church's established doctrine and to destroy any knowledge that challenges its authority. It is said that they are relentless in their pursuit, and that they have silenced many who dared to defy their will. I must remain ever vigilant, for they are a constant threat to the sacred truth I now bear.

My heart is heavy with the knowledge that, if discovered, the Order of Papal Guardians would stop at nothing to see the Gospel of St. Salome eradicated. It is my responsibility, therefore, to ensure its survival and to safeguard its teachings for future generations. I have consulted with trusted advisors, and we have begun to devise a plan to hide the Gospel in a place where it may be found by those who seek the truth, yet remain hidden from those who would see it destroyed.

In the meantime, I shall continue to study its teachings and incorporate its wisdom into my own leadership, subtly and cautiously. I hope that by doing so, I can sow the seeds of change and plant the ideas of love, compassion, and equality within the Church, even if I cannot openly proclaim the Gospel's existence.

I pray that future generations, who may come to read these words, will be watchful of the Order of Papal Guardians and their nefarious intentions. Let them be a reminder to always seek the truth, even when it is hidden, and to remain steadfast in the face of adversity. The future of the Church, and the salvation of all humanity, may well depend upon it."

Michael looked up at Robbie's mother with astonishment. "Victoria, I find it curious you mentioned this Order of Papal Guardians just yesterday! And if Lord Pelham is in fact a member, we must keep him from learning about this diary at all costs, and especially its reference to St. Salome's Gospel."

Returning to the diary, Michael turned the page, and as he did he noticed something odd, an unusual structure in the pages.

"Wait… there seems to be an integral leaf attached to this page. No, actually it's a sort of envelope. And there's another loose page of vellum inside…"

He removed the small, tightly folded document and

opened it carefully. It too was written in Old English, though in a different hand, and its author was unspecified.

After a few moments of silence as the priest read the vellum, he took a deep breath and looked around at the others. Without further introduction, he began reading...

"To uncover the Gospel of St. Salome, one must first locate the chapel within the Abbey where an underground altar is situated. This lesser-known altar, dedicated to a forgotten saint, was once used for quiet prayers and contemplation. Hidden from plain sight, it can be found by carefully studying the Abbey's floor plan or by consulting a knowledgeable guide.

From the Lady Chapel in Sherborne Abbey, a hidden passage lies concealed behind an ancient doorway adorned with intricate carvings of vines and flowers. A keen observer may notice a small, vine-entwined cross that appears out of place among the carvings. Pressing the center of the cross will reveal a secret compartment, containing a worn parchment with a riddle etched upon it. Having taken these steps already, I herewith lay out the riddle and the process of discovering the Gospel, which I allowed to remain in place:

> *'Seek the altar where holy prayers ascend,*
> *Yet not to heaven, but depths they wend,*
> *Find the place where the good saint rests,*
> *Three steps past her gaze, a hidden crest.'*

Upon finding the underground altar, search for the tomb of the good saint mentioned in the riddle. This tomb, adorned with a carved image of the saint, lies partially obscured by shadows. You may also notice a distinctive, worn crest covering most of the floor of this room.

From said tomb, take three steps in the direction the saint's eyes are gazing, then kneel down and feel the floor for any inconsistencies, and you will discover a hidden mechanism in the floor. Turn the mechanism to the right, and a small, hidden alcove will be revealed in the wall beside you. Within this concealed space, wrapped in a protective cloth, lies the long-lost Gospel of St. Salome, waiting to share its wisdom with the world once more."

"That must be the secret door that Lord Pelham vanished through the other day," Hana said. "I imagine it leads to the underground altar beneath the abbey this document mentions. We've got to go back now!"

"Settle down there, Cousin," Karl said with some caution. "If this Pelham character knows about the passageway and the underground altar, he may have already discovered the gospel and dealt with it. It may already be destroyed."

"I tend to doubt that, Karl," Michael declared, "since it's not likely there were many clues of this nature floating around. And we just discovered this one now. No, I would bet the gospel is still in its hiding place. But I do agree with Hana that we need to set out first thing tomorrow and check it out. Meanwhile, let's finish our reading here."

Michael flipped the page to the next entry, when suddenly, staring at the page, he blurted, "Good Lord! I just skipped ahead and it appears Joan had fallen in love! Listen to this…

"18th June 856, Rome —

I find myself in an emotional whirlwind, one that I never thought possible. My life has been consumed by a secret passion, a forbidden affection I cannot resist. I have fallen in love with a man who holds my heart and my secrets in his hands. His name is Alexander… Cardinal Alexander Rossini.

Alexander's eyes seem to pierce the very depths of my soul, and his touch sends shivers down my spine. Our love, though clandestine, fills me with a warmth that I have never known before. As a man of the cloth, his heart is torn between the duties he has sworn to uphold and the desires that burn so fiercely within him.

Alexander knows of my duplicity—the double life I've led, the lies I've whispered in the shadows. And yet, he loves me still. It is as if our souls are bound together, and despite the barriers that society has placed between us, we are drawn to each other like moths to a flame.

The passion we share in our stolen moments is a balm to the wounds that fester in the darkest corners of my heart. Alexander's touch is gentle, yet demanding, and it leaves me aching for more. In his arms, I feel as though I can finally be my true self—flawed, vulnerable, and utterly in love.

But the weight of our secret is a heavy burden to bear. We walk a precarious tightrope, and the threat of discovery looms over us like a dark cloud. As much as I long to shout our love from the rooftops, I know that doing so would bring ruin upon us both. We are bound by our oaths, and I cannot bear the thought of causing him to falter in his sacred duties.

Alexander and I know that our love may be doomed from the start, but we cannot help but hold onto it with every fiber of our being. As I lay my head down to rest, my heart aches with the knowledge that our love can only exist within these pages, locked away from the world.

Yet, despite the danger, I cannot help but dream of a day when Alexander and I might be free to love one another without fear or shame. Until that day comes, I shall hold our memories close to my heart, and I shall find solace in the knowledge that, at least for now, we are bound together by a love that transcends the boundaries of our earthly existence."

Midway through the passages as Michael was reading, Hana began to weep softly as she weighed each achingly impactful word, sympathetic to the predicament of this obviously determined yet tortured woman. And that she had found love inside the Church was doubly painful for Hana, who measured her own impossible situation in wistful comparison.

Looking up as she wiped her eyes, she saw Michael staring back at her, that familiar look of pensive melancholy in his gaze. She knew at that exact moment that he, too, recognized it.

What are we going to do? she agonized.

RETURNING TO THE DIARY, Michael flipped forward to the next pages, noting there were roughly two months since the previous entry and the one prior. As he sat silent, mentally translating from the Old English, his demeanor changed.

"You won't believe what she's written next… I expect this must have been what ended her papacy:

"4th August 857, Rome —

My heart is heavy with a secret that I can no longer keep hidden within these pages. The truth has taken root within me, and I feel both fear and wonder coursing through my veins. I am with child—a new life blossoms inside me, a testament to the love Alexander and I share. Yet, this miraculous gift also threatens to unravel the delicate threads that have held my world together.

As Pope, my duty is to be the shepherd of my flock, the spiritual leader of a vast and diverse congregation. My life is devoted to service, and I am bound by sacred vows that I have sworn to uphold. A child—our child—would shatter the façade of piety that has shielded me from suspicion and doubt.

The foreboding implications of my predicament are not lost on me. The whispers and rumors that would follow the revelation of my pregnancy would be a storm that I could not weather. The trust and respect of my followers would crumble, and the very foundation of my position would be shaken to its core.

Alexander and I have been so careful, so discreet in our clandestine encounters. Yet, we have been careless with the gift of love that has bloomed between us, and now I must face the consequences of our actions.

I find myself torn between the life growing within me and the life I have built as Pope. How can I reconcile these two worlds that seem destined to collide? How can I protect this innocent life, when doing so would risk the destruction of all that I have worked for?

My heart aches with the weight of the decision that lies before me. I know that, no matter what path I choose, I will be faced with loss and sorrow. But I also know that I must find the strength to face this challenge head-on, and to navigate the stormy waters that lie ahead.

In the quiet solitude of my chambers, I turn to prayer for guidance and solace. I pray for wisdom to make the right decision, for courage to face the consequences, and forgive-ness for the choices I have made.

As I close my eyes and seek comfort in the silence, I can only hope that the light of truth will illuminate the path before me, and guide me through the darkness that threatens to engulf my world."

CHAPTER
EIGHT

The sun had already set when Reverend Warren Andrews left his vicarage in Sherborne and drove to the upscale village of Lyme Regis on Dorset's Jurassic Coast. Turning onto the palm tree-lined drive leading to the seaside estate of Lord Lucius Pelham, the vicar parked his VW Passat on the gravel lot, then got out and nervously made his way to the main entry.

As he approached the grand house, the most impressive thing he noticed was its imposing presence, perched atop a gently sloping cliff with night-lit azure waves crashing against the rocky shore below. The aged brick and limestone exterior, adorned with ivy and climbing roses, hinted at the rich history and timeless elegance of the estate. The front entryway was nestled beneath an intricately carved portico supported by two stately Corinthian columns. The grand entrance featured a set of large, solid oak double doors, adorned with ornate, wrought-iron hinges and an antique brass knocker in the shape of a lion's head, symbolizing the nobility and power of the manor's owner, the current master of the ancient House of Pelham.

Gathering his courage, Andrews knocked on the door. Lucius Pelham was a capricious, temperamental sort, and the vicar never knew what mood the man would be in, especially when he called on him unbidden, despite the importance of the visit.

A butler opened the door. "Good evening, Reverend. Is His Lordship expecting you?"

"I did ring him earlier, Bertram, so yes, he knows I'm coming."

"Very good, sir. Please follow me to the drawing room." With a slight bow and a stiff smile, the butler took the vicar's coat and hat and hung them on a wall rack by the door.

Impeccably dressed in his morning coat, with tails neatly pressed and a white starched shirt underneath, the butler led the way down a grand hallway lined with tall windows looking out over Lyme Bay and the darkening English Channel beyond. The walls were painted a soft ivory, with intricate moldings and baseboards adding to the grandeur of the space. The floors were made of polished marble, with a rich red carpet running the length of the hallway. Along the walls were several dark oil paintings of past generations of the family, depicting noble ancestors in grand attire and austere countenance.

As they approached the drawing room, the butler stopped in front of a large wooden door with a brass knob. He pushed the door open and stepped aside, allowing the vicar to enter first to await Pelham's arrival. The drawing room was spacious, with high ceilings and a blazing fireplace taking center stage. The room was elegantly furnished in a classic English hunting motif, with plush sofas and chairs upholstered in luxurious fabrics, accented with tassels and fringe. The heads of various animals peered down from the walls, with wooden plaques depicting intricate details preserved in the taxidermy. The antlers of deer were prominently displayed, with light-brown tines branching out in every direction. The heads of wild boar showed off razor-sharp tusks, massive and savage even in death. The animals appeared to stare down at Andrews, their glassy eyes seemingly fixed on the happenings of the room. Despite being dead and mounted on the wall, the animals' powerful presence and ferocity seemed to linger in the air, adding an element of danger and intimidation.

"Would you care for a refreshment, Reverend? A smart cocktail, perhaps?"

In his low, raspy voice, Andrews replied gratefully, "Oh, indeed, Bertram, that would be lovely, yes. I'll have a double gin and tonic, please." Just what he needed to calm his nerves in this dreadful room of death as he anxiously awaited Pelham's arrival.

Some twenty minutes later, as Andrews was nearly finished with his drink, the door to the room burst open and Pelham hobbled in, his cane oddly tapping the floor several times, as if seeking firm purchase before leaning down on it as a support.

"Good evening, Reverend," the old man said wearily as he sat down in a chair by the fire, opposite Andrews. He made a point of looking at the clock over the fireplace, which read half-past seven. "I trust you have good reason to call on me at this late hour?"

"Yes, my apologies, Your Lordship, but..." Andrews

looked into the flames, searching for the right words. The gin had helped, yet still the words slipped out with a hesitancy that belied his uncertainty. "I happened to have overheard something in the abbey earlier, which I was certain you might wish to know at once."

He paused as the door opened quietly. Bertram entered holding a round silver serving tray, on which sat a brandy snifter containing an amber beverage which he placed on a wooden side table perched next to Pelham, who wordlessly gestured his acknowledgment with a slight wave of his hand.

"Go on," he said to Andrews as the butler left the room.

"Well, just a few hours ago I happened to be standing on the second-floor gallery over the Lady Chapel when Father Dominic and his colleagues, the, uh, visitors from the Vatican—" he hesitated but saw Pelham reveal no surprise at the mention of the name—"were visiting the abbey. I heard them talking about some riddle, and the name 'Pope Joan' came up, which caught my attention."

Pelham's eyes now opened wide and he sat forward. "*Pope Joan?!* Are you absolutely certain that's what you heard?"

"Without a doubt, sir. They mentioned the name several times. But then the most extraordinary thing happened. The riddle apparently contained the solution to a puzzle of sorts, one ultimately revealing a hidden compartment in the chapel which I never knew existed. Once they had gained access to a compartment beneath the Horsey tomb, they discovered an ancient book. I heard them talk about it as a diary, which I assumed belonged to this Pope Joan they spoke of. Of course, there never was a Pope Joan so far as I know, since—"

"Never mind that," Pelham interrupted abruptly. "What have they done with the *book?* Did you just let them take it from the abbey without interfering?"

Andrews' mouth dropped open, then closed, before he answered, "Your Lordship, I was trying to stay out of sight, hoping to get as much information as I could for you when—"

"You fool!" he cut in again, this time angrily. "You should have demanded that book be turned over to you at once! It is the property of Sherborne Abbey, not meddlers from the Vatican." Pelham's intense gaze pierced right through Andrews, a steely and unrelenting focus with a hint of dread and menace lurking just below the surface, one that made it clear he was not to be trifled with. "So, what else did you overhear while quivering in the shadows like some timorous chambermaid?"

Reverend Andrews was mortified. His next words tumbled out of him. "They... they started reading the diary, and discovered that her surname was 'Anglicus,' the very same as the Anglicus family of Saxon Hall. In fact, young Robert was among Father Dominic's entourage, and he seemed quite excited by the presumed relationship.

"Anyway, Dominic began reading an entry in the diary. It evidently confirmed that this Pope Joan was in fact a real person who led the Church in the ninth century, having hidden herself under the guise of a man for God knows how long. Do you realize what this means, Your Lordship? If true, it is obviously a significant rewriting of history for the Catholic Church!"

Pelham was silent. The muscles in his face twitched involuntarily as he considered what to do with this knowledge—and more ominously, what to do with the vicar, who should never have learned what he'd overheard.

~

HAVING REFRESHED his teacup with hot Earl Grey, Michael continued reading to the others…

"22nd June 873, Sherborne, England —

It has been many years since I last put pen to these pages, and my life has taken a course I could never have predicted. After the harrowing exposure of my pregnancy and the regrettably public birth of my son while in procession on Rome's Via Sacra, the people turned vicious, casting stones at both me and my infant child. Were it not for my guards hastening our departure to the palace, we would surely have died on the spot. Alexander bravely but secretly arranged for our furtive escape from the Vatican that very night, lest we be killed or imprisoned by my enemies. My heart was heavy with sorrow, but I knew it was a necessary sacrifice to protect my child and the Church to which I had devoted my life.

In the aftermath of my departure, I left Rome and found secret solace in the picturesque Saxon countryside of Sherborne in Dorset, England, the ancestral home of my family. It was here, in the embrace of verdant hills and endless skies, that I started my life anew. I named my son Gregory, and he is a constant reminder of the love Alexander and I shared, and of the strength and resilience that had carried me through the darkest of times.

As I watch Gregory grow, I cherish each moment of laughter and wonder, and I endeavor to instill in him the values of love, compassion, and wisdom. My heart swells with pride as he blossoms into a thoughtful and caring young man, a beacon of hope in a world that has often seemed steeped in shadows.

In the years that followed my abdication, Alexander ascended to the papacy and took the name Pope John VIII. In a poignant act of devotion, he chose to honour my own regnal name, a gesture that spoke volumes of the love that still burned between us. Even though the Church had stricken my name from its records and sought to erase my existence, Alexander's choice was a powerful testament to our bond, a secret whispered between two souls bound by fate.

Though oceans and responsibilities separate us, the love Alexander and I share remains as steadfast as the day we first met. We exchange letters filled with words of love and longing, each one a lifeline that tethers us together despite the distance. We dream of a day when we might be reunited, when the weight of our duties will no longer keep us apart.

Meanwhile, my days in Dorset are filled with quiet contentment, a balm to the tumultuous life I had once led. I find solace in the simple pleasures of tending my garden and watching the seasons change, and in the knowledge that, though my life had taken an unexpected turn, I have found a haven of peace in which to raise my beloved son."

Turning to the next entry, which appeared to be two years later, Michael kept reading…

"2nd September 875, Sherborne —

Today, I received news that fills my heart with a mixture of pride and trepidation. Alexander, as Pope John VIII, has appointed our son Gregory as the Bishop of Ostia. The news arrived in a letter penned by Alexander himself, his words brimming with joy and affection.

I cannot help but feel an immense sense of pride as I think of Gregory, the child born of our love, taking up such a prestigious position within the Church. His journey from the rolling hills of Dorset to the hallowed halls of Ostia has been a testament to his intelligence, dedication, and the unwavering faith that guides him.

However, beneath the pride there is a current of unease that gnaws at me. In elevating Gregory to the rank of bishop, Alexander has drawn him closer to the very heart of the Church—and to the secrets that lie buried in our past. I cannot help but worry that Gregory's newfound prominence may attract unwanted scrutiny, and that our carefully guarded secrets may be brought to light.

The thought of Gregory bearing the burden of our transgressions weighs heavily on my heart. I have spent a lifetime seeking to protect him from the shadows of my past, and I cannot bear the thought that my actions may have inadvertently placed him in harm's way.

Yet, in spite of my fears, I must remind myself of the strength and resilience that have carried us through the darkest of times. Gregory is a young man of unwavering conviction and boundless compassion, and I have no doubt that he will serve the Church with honour and grace.

As I sit in the quiet solitude of my Dorset cottage, my thoughts turn to Alexander and the love that has sustained us through the years. Though we are separated by distance and circumstance, our bond remains unbroken—a testament to the power of love to transcend the boundaries that the world imposes upon us.

And so, I choose to place my trust in the fates, and to believe that the path before us is one that has been divinely ordained. With courage in our hearts and faith as our guide, we will face whatever challenges lie ahead, and we will find solace in the knowledge that our love has given us the strength to endure."

And the next entry, seven years later, left the group with profound sadness. Michael read on...

"23rd December 882, Sherborne —

I write with a heart shattered by grief, my soul plunged into the depths of despair. The news of Alexander's fate has reached me, a cruel reminder of the fragility of life and the cost of love. My Alexander, the man who held my heart and the father of our son, has been assassinated by his own Curia. The very men who should have been his closest allies and protectors have betrayed him in the most heinous of ways. I am told he was first poisoned, and then, when the poison failed to claim his life, they brutally clubbed him to death.

The pain of his loss is unbearable, a maelstrom of anguish that threatens to consume me. My world, once filled with hope and love, now lies in ruins, and I am left to pick up the pieces of a shattered existence. I feel as though a part of me has been ripped away, leaving a void that can never be filled.

The injustice of Alexander's demise fills me with a burning rage, a desire for vengeance that courses through my veins. And yet, I know that such thoughts are futile, for they cannot bring him back to me, nor can they mend the broken fragments of my heart.

In this darkest hour, I turn to prayer for solace, seeking refuge in the comforting embrace of faith. I pray for Alexander's soul, that he may find peace in the arms of the Divine. I pray for our son, Gregory, that he may have the strength to bear the weight of this terrible loss. And I pray for myself, that I may find the courage to carry on in a world without the man who was my anchor and my guiding light.

Through the haze of grief, I know that he would want me to honour his memory, not by succumbing to despair, but by living a life filled with love and compassion.

And so, I shall strive to do just that. I shall cherish the memories of the time we spent together, and I shall carry the love we shared in my heart, a beacon of hope in the darkness. I shall dedicate myself to our son, ensuring that he, too, carries forth the legacy of love and wisdom that Alexander embodied.

And in doing so, I shall keep alive the flame of our passion, a testament to the indomitable spirit of the human heart."

The priest looked up and around at the others. Each of them, enraptured in the telling, were spellbound by what they had heard, imagining the kind of life this courageous woman must have led. As Michael turned to the final pages, he said simply, "And this appears to be the last entry, some five years later...

"4th May 887, Sherborne —

As I sit in the quiet solitude of my home, I feel the inexorable march of time and the steady approach of my own mortality. My body has grown weak, and my spirit, once a raging fire, has been tempered by the winds of age. The end of my journey draws near, and I find myself reflecting on the tapestry of my life—the triumphs and tragedies, the love and loss that have defined my existence.

My years as Pope, though marked by the shadows of deceit and secrecy, were a testament to the strength of the human spirit and the resilience of the heart. I defied the conventions of the time and rose to a position of power that few could have imagined possible, especially women. I navi-

gated the treacherous waters of politics and faith, and I did so with a steadfast determination to serve my flock and uphold the values I held dear.

In Alexander, I found the love of a lifetime, a mate to my soul who understood my heart and my ambitions in a way that no one else ever could. Our love, though forbidden and fraught with danger, was a beacon of hope that guided me through the darkest moments of my life. The memories of our time together are etched into my heart, a testament to the power of love to transcend the boundaries of this mortal existence.

In raising our son, Gregory, I discovered a wellspring of joy and pride that I had never known before. I watched him grow into a wise and compassionate man, a leader who carried forth the legacy of the love that Alexander and I shared. As Bishop of Ostia, he has served the Church with honour and grace, and I know that he will continue to do so long after I am gone.

As I prepare to leave this world, I have chosen to entrust my story—the story of my life, my loves, and my heartache—to the hallowed walls of Sherborne Abbey. It is here that I will secret away this diary, a record of my most cherished memories and my deepest sorrows. Perhaps one day, someone will discover these pages and come to know the woman who dared to defy the odds, to serve the Church with honour, and to love without fear or regret.

As I face the unknown, I am comforted by the knowledge that my life has not been lived in vain. I have loved fiercely, I have fought bravely, and I have left a legacy that will endure long after I am gone. And in the twilight of my life, I find solace in the belief that Alexander and I will be reunited once more, our souls entwined in the eternal embrace of love."

The priest closed the diary, his hands trembling slightly from the weight of the emotions conjured by the words. He looked around the room, and he could see that he was not the only one who had been moved by the story of this remarkable woman. Despite the hardships she endured, Joan had found the courage to keep going, driven by a love that refused to be extinguished.

And as he thought about her legacy, he realized that she had left behind something more than just memories. She had left behind a message of hope, a testament to the strength of the human spirit and the power of love to endure. Michael knew that he would never forget the story of Joan Anglicus, and he made a silent promise to carry her message with him always. For in a world that could be so dark and cruel, her words were a beacon of light, a reminder that even in the face of tragedy, love could conquer all.

He looked up at Hana. Clearly, she too had experienced the same passionate grounding from what she'd heard. They furtively exchanged a longing glance, then each looked away, unprepared to let the others witness their mutual emotions, revealing something more than might otherwise be assumed.

CHAPTER
NINE

T he thick, heavy door creaked open as Bertram led Cardinal Bennett Dreyfus into the dimly lit office of Lord Lucius Pelham. Dreyfus strode in, his tall frame filling the doorway as he cast a disdainful glance around the room. As with most such spaces in Pelham's centuries-old manor, it was filled with ancient tomes, antique furniture and faded tapestries, a testament to the rich history of the area his family had called home for generations.

Dreyfus's eyes came to rest on Lucius Pelham himself, a terse but frail-looking man with a deeply furrowed brow, seated at the desk in the room. The green, glass-shaded desk lamp next to him cast dramatic shadows on his face, making him seem even more gaunt than usual.

"Ah, Cardinal," Pelham greeted him, nodding his head with respect. "Thank you for joining me. I was just going through these documents, researching our esteemed Order's stance on women in the Church."

Dreyfus took the seat across from Pelham, the latter's gaze fixed on the elderly cardinal. "Indeed, Your Lordship. Yes, I imagine this discovery of Pope Joan's diary you mentioned on the phone might have prompted such a review. It is a conviction that the Order of Papal Guardians has defended for centuries, even as society has changed around us. Our opposition to women serving in high roles in the Church, especially as pope, is rooted in both tradition and practicality."

Pelham nodded in agreement, his fingers shuffling the documents laid out before him. "Of course, the tradition is clear. The Church's foundations are built upon the teachings of Christ and apostolic succession. Jesus chose twelve men to be his apostles, and the first bishops were men as well. The priesthood has always been a male domain."

"Exactly," Dreyfus concurred, his voice cold and dismissive. "The apostolic lineage has been passed down from St. Peter to his successors, an unbroken chain of male popes with the single exception of that fraudulent interloper, the Popess Joan. To further allow a woman to serve in such a role would stain that sacred lineage, undermining the very foundations of our faith. Women simply do not have the same capacity for leadership as men, especially in spiritual matters.

"But—playing devil's advocate here for a moment— surely you recognize that women have made significant contributions to the Church throughout history? Saints like Catherine of Siena and Teresa of Ávila come to mind. They were not only spiritual leaders but also valued advisors to popes and kings."

Pelham scoffed at the suggestion. "Cardinal, those women were exceptions, not the rule. Yes, they were able to serve God and the Church in their own unique ways, but without compromising the apostolic succession or the male priesthood. We cannot let a few outliers dictate the policies of our entire Church."

"I understand your point, Lord Pelham," Dreyfus sighed, his gaze drifting towards an oil painting on the wall depicting the Last Supper. "But, we do live in a modern world that has seen women rise to prominent positions in all walks of life, including politics and business. Is it not possible that the Church, too, can adapt to these changing times and allow women to serve in higher roles?"

Pelham's expression darkened. "The Church is not a secular institution, Eminence. Its purpose is not to conform to the whims of society but to preserve and transmit the teachings of Christ. We cannot simply change our beliefs and practices to appease the demands of the modern world. The Church has faced countless challenges throughout its history, from schisms to heresies, but it has always remained steadfast in its convictions. Women simply have no place in our Church's hierarchy."

Dreyfus nodded slowly. "Yes, I see your point and agree we must remain faithful to our beliefs, even if it means standing against the tide of popular opinion."

Pelham leaned in closer, his eyes narrowing. "There is another reason, Cardinal Dreyfus, that we must not overlook. The Church, as a hierarchical institution, requires order and discipline to function effectively. Allowing women to serve in high roles would introduce chaos and disorder among the faithful."

Dreyfus looked up, his eyes searching Pelham's face. "How so, Lord Pelham?"

"Consider the challenges we already face in maintaining the unity of the Church," Pelham continued. "We must navigate a complex array of cultural, political, and linguistic differences among our global congregation. Introducing women into the hierarchy would exacerbate these divisions, especially in more conservative regions where the idea of female leadership remains controversial."

Dreyfus nodded, his brow furrowed with concern. "Yes, you've posed another valid point. The Church must be a beacon of stability and continuity in an ever-changing world. If we were to permit women to serve in high roles, we could risk alienating a significant and more conservative portion of our flock."

"Indeed, Eminence," Pelham agreed. "We must not forget the practical implications of such a change. The Church's infrastructure and customs have been built around the male priesthood. Everything from the design of our sacred vestments to the language of our liturgy reflects this reality. To accommodate women in high roles would necessitate a sweeping reevaluation of our traditions and practices, a disruption that could further weaken our already fragile unity."

Dreyfus sighed. "It is a heavy burden we bear, Lord Pelham, to preserve the integrity of our faith in the face of mounting pressures."

Pelham's expression remained cold and unyielding. "It is, yes. But it is a responsibility that we, as leaders of the Order of Papal Guardians, must shoulder with unwavering resolve. We have been entrusted with the sacred duty of safeguarding the Church's teachings and traditions, even when they are challenged by the shifting sands of time."

Dreyfus looked into Pelham's eyes, his expression resolute. "You are right, Lord Pelham. We must stand firm in our convictions, no matter how difficult the path may be."

With a solemn nod, Pelham rose from his seat, grabbing his cane. "Together, Eminence, we will ensure that the Church remains true to its divine purpose, guided by the wisdom of its male leaders and the largely unbroken chain of apostolic succession. To that end, we must acquire the popess's diary at once and suppress the damage it has already generated.

"We have other cleanup duties to attend to as well."

CHAPTER
TEN

T he next day everyone gradually awoke to the most amazing smells emanating from the kitchen. Having arrived hours earlier, Victoria's cook, Mrs. Agnes Whitmore, had prepared a "fry-up" for her lady's guests, a hearty and traditional British meal typically consisting of a variety of cooked items: scrambled eggs, streaky bacon, pork sausages called bangers, black pudding—a type of blood sausage made from pork blood and fat with a filler of barley or oatmeal—grilled tomatoes, a fresh mushroom medley sautéed in butter, "bubble and squeak"—a dish made from fried leftover vegetables, in this case potatoes and cabbage—baked beans, toast with marmalades, jams and Marmite spreads, and a selection of juices, tea and coffee, plus various condiments.

Karl and Lukas made it downstairs first and were overtaken by the aromas of what was obviously a feast laid on for their benefit.

"This is amazing, Victoria! Did you do all this your-self?" Lukas asked.

"Heavens, no, dear boy. I hardly had a hand in it at all, apart from making the coffee, a task at which I excel," she said, winking at the young Swiss Guard. "No, this is all the doing of our beloved Mrs. Whitmore. A proper full English breakfast for everyone to start your day off right." She poured coffee into two mugs and slid them over to both boys.

The others ambled downstairs over the next twenty minutes, all with similar reactions Lukas and Karl had when smelling, then seeing, all the tempting foods.

"Mrs. Whitmore, you must come back to the Vatican with us and cook for a hundred and thirty Swiss Guards, all of whom would be thrilled to have you," Karl said enthusiastically. "And we're always hungry!"

The plump Englishwoman blushed and grinned with pride as she brought her apron up to wipe her forehead, then vainly tried coaxing resistant wisps of stray hair back into place atop her head.

Gathered around the large dining table, everyone chattered about various topics as bowls and plates were passed around, but as they were nearing the time to leave the conversation naturally turned back to the Gospel of St. Salome.

"I'm so excited about what we'll find next that it's hard to contain myself," Hana said as she pushed back her chair and passed a hand over her stomach. "Speaking of which, if one more forkful passes my lips, I'll burst. Thank you for such a lovely and sumptuous feast, Victoria. That was a perfect start to our day."

Michael was heading back to his room to change for

the day's outing when his phone rang. He didn't recognize caller ID but saw it was a local Dorset number.

"This is Michael Dominic," he answered.

"Father Dominic, Lord Pelham here. Am I to understand correctly that you found some sort of ancient diary in Sherborne Abbey?" He left little room for argument with such a direct question, but Michael was already taken off guard.

"Well, I... uh, I'm not really sure what you mean, Your Lordship." Rolling his eyes, even Michael didn't believe his own response, one crafted on the spur of the moment. Should he admit the truth, or hedge for time?

"I was led to believe you discovered a diary in the hand of some female pretender to the papal throne, of all things. I would certainly like to get that from you if so, since it is the property of Sherborne. When can you have it delivered to me?"

Well, that's certainly presumptuous, Michael thought. He let silence fill the gap.

"Come now, Father... I have it on good authority that you are in possession of that which does not belong to you, and I insist you turn it over to me at once!"

"Lord Pelham, I see no reason for doing any such thing," Michael protested. "At great effort, we were guided to that discovery by independent manuscripts not belonging to the abbey, then were prompted to solve a series of arcane clues and ancient devices in order to expose the resting place of a book that's been in hiding for centuries. It's as much the property of the Holy Roman Catholic Church, written by the hand of a Catholic as it is anyone's, for that matter, and as prefect of the Vatican Apostolic Archives, I claim the book on behalf of the Church."

There was a pause of such building resentment that Michael could feel it in the dreadful silence. "Are you quite certain that is your final word on the matter, Dominic?" Pelham asked, his rage now incandescent. "There *will* be consequences, I assure you!" Michael could hear the angry spittle hitting Pelham's mouthpiece as he sputtered out the words.

"Then I don't see we have anything further to discuss," the priest said flatly.

The line went dead as Pelham disconnected the call.

WITH ALL SIX OF THEM—ROBBIE, Michael, Hana, Aaron, Karl and Lukas—settled into Robbie's spacious Land Rover, they made their way back through the rolling green hills of the English countryside and on into Sherborne. They rode mostly in silence, each fully sated from breakfast and pondering what lay ahead for them that day.

There were no other cars in the abbey's graveled parking lot so Robbie parked the SUV nearest the main entrance. They all got out and made for the large double oak doors. Surprisingly, they found them locked.

"That's odd," Robbie said. "The sign here says it should be open now. Let's try another door."

Making their way around the left side of the abbey, Karl was the first to reach a smaller door, which he found to be unlocked. Opening it, he let the others enter before following them in.

As their eyes adjusted to the stark difference in lighting, they walked through the empty main chapel and back toward the smaller Lady Chapel at the far east end of the building. Once there, Hana, reaching it first, found and opened the door to the secret passageway they had seen Lord Pelham walk through two days earlier. She led the way for the others, keen to see where this curious passage would take them.

The passageway itself was very narrow, lit by a string of small LED lights fastened along the center of the low arched ceiling. Just up ahead on the left, Hana saw a short flight of stone steps leading downward. Grasping the old iron railing, she turned and stepped down, continuing until she reached a wooden door. She opened it.

The cold, musty room beyond was fairly small, with a low ceiling and a modest, ancient stone altar at the opposite end from where they had entered. Against the side wall was the tomb of the "good saint" mentioned in the riddle, though otherwise unnamed. Michael—who had photographed the vellum so he wouldn't have to chance harming the original—opened his iPhone and again read the riddle instructions aloud to the others.

"... *This tomb, adorned with a carved image of the saint, lies partially obscured by shadows. From the tomb, take three steps in the direction the saint's eyes are gazing, and you will find yourself in a dim room with a distinctive, worn crest covering most of the floor. Kneel and feel the floor for any inconsistencies, and you will discover a hidden mechanism within the crest. Turn the mechanism to the right, and a small, hidden alcove will be revealed in the wall beside you...*"

"Well, yes, there's the crest. I can make it out now," Hana noted, looking down at the large but terribly faded insignia on the floor. Moving forward to the carved effigy of the saint above the tomb, she took three paces in the direction of the saint's gaze, which was staring slightly to Hana's right, then knelt down and slid her hand across the stone floor.

"There *is* something here!" she said with excitement, her hand finding a circular segment of stone with two slight indentations where fingers could be used to turn it. But getting it to move at all was a challenge.

"Karl, could you give me a hand with this? Or better yet, just two strong fingers will do," she said, grinning.

"You bet," her cousin replied, dropping to his knees and applying more pressure with his hand as his thumb and middle finger did their best to grab hold of the slightly indented hollows and turn the mechanism clockwise. With effort, it began to move.

And as it turned, the crack of a hidden alcove started to appear in the wall beside where Hana now stood. "It's working, Karl! Keep going!" she said, cheering him on. Grunting as he put his back into it, he'd turned it enough that the opening was now sufficient to reach inside—which Hana did with fervid anticipation.

In her hands was a length of old quilted cloth protecting a folded parchment which lay within, its dark, age-worn corners poking out through the cloth.

"That looks like gambeson," Michael said. "Amazing. Gambeson was a reinforced quilted padding used mainly in place of armor. It actually preceded armor in the Middle Ages. During the tenth century, gambeson evolved and became more widespread as a form of defensive clothing. It provided protection against various types of attacks, including cuts, thrusts, and blunt force. But as we see here, it was also used to protect precious items from damage—such as whatever it is you're holding but not showing us…" He grinned as his elbow lightly pushed against Hana. "So? *What's inside?!*"

"Oh… right! I was utterly taken in by this whole fascinating experience. Spooky secret passageways. Mysterious instructions. Hidden mechanisms and sliding alcoves. I mean, what's a girl to do with all this?"

"A girl should share what she's holding, *that's* what!"

"You do it, Michael." She handed the gambeson-wrapped packet to the priest, who accepted it with due reverence. "It probably needs your translation anyway."

Just as he was about to unfold the quilted cloth, they all heard the unmistakable sound of a distant door slamming shut echoing through the secret passage.

Lukas and Karl ran to the door of the room they were in, their heads peering out into the now pitch black passageway.

"The overhead lights have been turned off," Karl whispered. "And I suspect somebody may have been listening to us."

"Let's not take a chance on having to yield this gospel to anyone just yet," Michael cautioned, slipping the gambeson-covered parchment into his backpack. "I say we return to Saxon Hall now and read it there."

"Agreed," said Hana. "It's cold and eerie down here anyway, and the mere thought of someone spying on us isn't all that comforting."

With Karl taking the vanguard position and Lukas assuming rearguard, they each removed their iPhones, turned on the flashlight app, and lit the way forward up the steps of the passageway and back into the Lady Chapel, ever cautious for a surprise attack from unseen combatants.

As the group emerged into the bright chapel through the concealed door, morning sunlight streamed through the magnificent stained glass windows, bathing the interior in a kaleidoscope of vibrant colors and casting a warm, ethereal glow on the stone floor and walls, a dramatic difference from the dim space they had just left.

Looking around, Karl found the chapel to be as empty as when they left it a short time earlier. But as he moved toward the tomb of Sir John and Lady Margaret Horsey, he noticed Reverend Warren Andrews, dressed in full ceremonial vestments and lying on top of the effigies of the knight and his lady, as if taking a nap, his hands clasped together in prayer.

Moving closer, Karl felt something was not right about this, not least of which was the man lying on top of the effigies.

Bending over him, Karl placed two fingers on the man's throat, feeling for a pulse.

There was none. Reverend Andrews was dead.

CHAPTER

ELEVEN

"Well, this was unexpected," Aaron said. "I don't think you need to worry about returning that diary now, Mikey."

The priest frowned at his all-too-practical friend with mild reprove. "Too soon, Aaron. I didn't know the man, but he at least deserves a few moments of respect." Michael stood over Andrews, silently praying the *Requiem Aeternam* as he asked for repose of the departed soul. He could not help but reflect on the melancholy he had witnessed in the man when they first met him. *What burden had he carried?* Michael wondered.

Meanwhile, Karl had already confirmed the vicar could not be revived, and now he was trying to figure out what, or who, may have killed him. Meanwhile, Lukas inspected the Lady Chapel for clues.

"Could he have taken his own life?" Hana asked. "He did appear sad when we first met him the other day. And by the look of him now, he does seem to be at peace. But

I do find it strange that he laid down on top of the effigies, don't you?"

"No," Karl said confidently, "Reverend Andrews was clearly murdered. Look here…" He pointed to the vicar's hands clasped in prayer, then pulled back the vestment sleeves he'd spied earlier. "See? His wrists have been bound together with a cincture cord, holding them in place in a prayerful position. Now, why would someone take the trouble of doing that? No, this is some kind of ritual symbolism. And he had to have been placed here within the last thirty minutes, since that's when we passed through the chapel on our way down to the underground altar—and he wasn't here then. Too, someone else was responsible for that slamming door and turning out the lights in the passage."

As Karl continued to inspect the body, Michael stood up and turned to face Hana. He placed a comforting hand on her shoulder, sensing her unease, as she cast glances about the corners of the room, as if anticipating the murderer was still lingering nearby.

Michael said, "It appears he was killed elsewhere and brought here, perhaps as a message. There are no signs of a struggle, no blood anywhere. And we would have surely heard a scuffle since the underground altar is right below the Lady Chapel. So the killer is long gone by now."

"A message?" Hana asked, intrigued.

"Yes," Michael said. "I have a feeling that whoever is responsible for this wanted us to find him here. There's something going on that we don't understand yet. I can't be sure, but I think it's related to our presence here in the abbey. And maybe even just being in Dorset at all, for that matter. Given Lord Pelham's angry call, and how we witnessed Andrews cower in the face of Pelham's outburst when we first arrived, I wouldn't be surprised if it was Reverend Andrews who told him we had the diary, though who knows how he found out." Michael looked around and above them, making a mental note of the second-floor landing above the Lady Chapel.

Karl looked up from the body. "I found something," he said, holding up a small, circular object with the hem of his jacket sleeve so as not to destroy any evidence. "It looks like some kind of medallion."

Michael looked closely at the object gripped between Karl's clothed fingers and examined it closely. "I've seen this symbol before," he said, pointing to an etching on the medallion of a serpent swallowing its own tail. "It's the Ouroboros, an ancient symbol used in various cultures throughout history. It typically represents the cyclical nature of life, death, and rebirth, as well as the eternal cycle of creation and destruction. It can also represent the idea of constant renewal, self-sufficiency, and the eternal return, as the snake continually consumes and renews itself in an endless loop.

"But note that the reverse side has the initials 'OPG' embossed on it beneath a papal tiara. Anyone care to venture a guess as to what that signifies?"

"My God!" Hana said at once. "The Order of Papal Guardians?"

"I'd say if it wasn't, it's an awfully strange coincidence. But the question is, did Reverend Andrews take the medallion as a clue to his murderer, or was it placed there by someone as a warning, or perhaps some sort of signature? Or could he have been a member himself?"

Hana looked at the medallion and wondered aloud,

"But why would the Order want Reverend Andrews dead?"

"I'm not sure," Michael said. "But I suspect we'll soon find out. Meanwhile, we should call the Dorset Police and report this, then head back to Saxon Hall and explore this Gospel of Salome. I think it's best we just tell them we're tourists wanting to see the abbey and its historic Lady Chapel. And we'll just leave out our prior visit, Pope Joan's diary, and especially the Salome Gospel. For now, the less we say, the better."

DETECTIVE INSPECTOR GRACE DEMPSEY arrived with a sizable entourage of additional officers in various panda cars and official vans, including crime scene investigators clad in white Tyvek personal protective coveralls nicknamed "bunny suits," along with several uniformed constables for crowd control. It seemed, in fact, that a large segment of the Dorset Police Department had shown up, especially since anything happening to the vicar of Sherborne Abbey would surely make the news, and everyone wanted a piece of that.

But Dempsey was clearly in charge.

"So, Father Michael Dominic, is it?" she asked with a melodic Gaelic accent, looking down at her notebook. "I'm DI Grace Dempsey. May I ask what brings you to Sherborne Abbey this morning, Father?"

"Ah, my mother's name was Grace," Michael said cheerfully.

"Is that a fact?" Dempsey said nonplussed, without looking up from her notes.

"It is, yes. Anyway, my friends and I just wanted to

see the historic abbey and its famed Lady Chapel. We're here from the Vatican as tourists enjoying the best Dorset has to offer—until this unfortunate discovery, of course."

"Can you tell me how you found the body? Where were you and what were you doing at the time?"

Michael gritted his teeth, working the muscles in his jaw. He absolutely hated lying. But to reveal their real activities that morning—not to mention the discovery of an ancient, world-class artifact—would serve no practical purpose. He would have quite a tale for the confessional when he got back to the Vatican.

"We were exploring the abbey itself, and when we wandered back through to the Lady Chapel, well, that's when we saw the vicar's body lying there atop the effigies. One of our Swiss Guards, Sergeant Karl Dengler, checked for a pulse but it was clear he was already dead. I said a prayer for him, then we called you. Oh, and the doors to the abbey were locked when we arrived, and Karl discovered a strange medallion on the body, which he left where he found it."

"The door was locked? Well, then, how did *you* get in?"

"Karl found a side door unlocked and open, so we went in that way."

Dempsey now gave Michael a piercing look, her instincts alert to something.

"So what I'm hearing is, despite the main door being locked, you decided to find a way in regardless?"

"As it happens, the posted sign out front showed the abbey should have been open then, so we didn't think it was important... like maybe someone just forgot to unlock it this morning, and with the side door being unlocked, well..."

Deciding this was logical, Dempsey relented. "If you don't mind then, please step over here and the constables will take a statement from each of you. Are you planning to leave Dorset any time soon, Father?"

"Actually, I have business at the British Museum in London on Tuesday, so we will be leaving tomorrow, then three of us will be flying back to Rome a couple days later. The Swiss Guards are on holiday and have their own vehicle, but I think they're heading back to Rome from here.

"Oh, and here's my card if you need to contact me for any reason." He reached inside his jacket pocket and retrieved one of his business cards, handing it to her.

"Fine," Dempsey said flatly, fingering the embossed, gold and silver papal coat of arms on the card. "In the meantime, Father, if you think of anything else you might remember, or that you'd like to tell me, here's *my* card." She already had her business card palmed and handed it to Michael, who slipped it in his pocket, trying not to look at the officer's eyes. He was once told *never* to make prolonged eye contact with a cop—something about animal instincts and perceived aggression—and the lesson stuck.

IT WAS JUST past noon when Robbie's Land Rover pulled up onto the front drive of Saxon Hall and discharged its passengers. The main thing on everyone's mind now was Michael's reading of the Gospel of St. Salome, so without a word said everyone filed into the library and took their customary seats, as they did when Michael read Pope Joan's diary.

As he fell back into his plush leather chair by the window, Michael took a deep breath to balance himself, then extracted the gambeson from his backpack and folded back its quilted cover. While white cotton gloves were traditionally used for handling rare books, manuscripts, and some ancient parchments, current best practices in the field of archival and conservation work often recommended not using gloves for these materials, since they can reduce tactile sensitivity and dexterity, potentially leading to accidental damage when handling delicate pages or bindings.

The folded parchment inside beckoned his attention like few things ever had. Despite dealing with the rarest of rare manuscripts in the Vatican, very few documents had survived from first-century Judea—specifically in and around the time of Christ—and at no time prior had anything ever been discovered in the hand of Salome, so the priest found himself treading new and exceedingly reverential ground. After all, it wasn't every day one could be the first to read the original writings of one of Jesus Christ's closest companions.

Carefully unfolding the small rectangular parchment packet, his hands trembling slightly, Michael first noticed the small, neatly formed glyphs comprising the Syrian dialect of the ancient Aramaic language—the Semitic language of Christ.

Michael looked up at the collective faces waiting for him to begin.

"Okay, here goes," he said, proceeding to read in a mildly labored, staccato-like cadence as he translated each successive word...

"In the name of the Father, the Son, and the Holy Spirit, I, Salome, a disciple of Christ and witness to His ministry, write these words as a testament to the true teachings He imparted upon us. Let this gospel serve as a guiding light for all who seek the truth and yearn for a deeper understanding of His divine message.

And so it came to pass that Jesus spoke to us, His followers, saying, 'Fear not the judgment of men, for they have conjured the notion of sin to wield power and control over others. True sin lies not in the transgressions they claim, but in the darkness of the heart—greed, cruelty, and the thirst for dominion over one's brethren.

'Heed my words, for I bring to you a message of love, compassion, and forgiveness. The Kingdom of God is within you, and it is through these virtues that you shall unlock the gates and enter into everlasting life.

'The teachings that have been recorded by others have been tainted by the hands of men seeking to maintain their own influence and dominion. They have obscured the truth, distorting my message to serve their own interests.

'I call upon you to reject the dogmas that have been built upon fear and repression. Do not shackle yourselves to the commandments of men, for it is through love, not fear, that you shall come to know the true essence of God.'

In the early days of the Church, men and women served as equals in leadership and ministry. I, Salome, was among the first to follow Jesus, and I bore witness to His teachings alongside my sisters and brothers. Do not be led astray by those who claim that women have no place within the Church, for they speak falsely.

The true Church is not bound by walls nor governed by the decrees of men. It is a living, breathing community of

*believers, united by their love for one another and their
commitment to the teachings of Christ. In the eyes of the
Lord, there is no division among His children—neither by
race, gender, nor social status.*

*I beseech you, my brothers and sisters, to seek the truth
within your own hearts and embrace the teachings that I
have shared with you. Let the light of Christ guide your path,
and may your love for one another be the beacon that leads
you to the Kingdom of God.*

Amen.

Salome of Jerusalem"

The room was dead silent when Michael finished. For
his part, he just kept staring at the page, his mind soaring
with the incongruity of everything he had been taught
about sin, and about the Church's traditional leadership
roles and its supposed authority over the hearts and
minds of a billion souls worldwide.

Karl in particular looked extremely uncomfortable,
shifting restlessly in his chair as he struggled with what
he had just heard.

In his typical droll fashion, Aaron asked the obvious
question. "Did anyone else catch that bit about, you
know, *'Fear not the judgment of men, for they have conjured
the notion of sin to wield power and control over others'*? That
seems pretty radical to me, in the sense that the broader
concept of 'sin' has been a given for over two thousand
years. Are we now to believe they got it wrong?"

"It would appear so," Michael said, reflexively
accepting the tenets of this clearly historical specimen
having the provenance of a pope, albeit one apparently
struck from the record. "You got it right, Aaron. This has

the power to radically change our entire view of sin and what it means to be a Christian. I'm just... totally overwhelmed by this. And I'm more than curious to hear what the Holy Father will have to say on the matter."

As always, Hana was impressed with Michael's modest use of the pope's formal titles, without referring to him as his own father.

But she had noticed something else in what Salome had written... something akin to what Pope Joan had said in her own diary. "Did you listen to that part about, *'Do not be led astray by those who claim that women have no place within the Church...'*? Wouldn't that be the entire Curia, Michael? Maybe the Holy Father could do something about that, too."

Michael was silent and reflective at first. Then, "While philosophically I agree with what I just heard in Salome's words—indeed, apparently also in the words of Christ Himself—we must understand that, until now, this message had either not been discovered for over two thousand years, or it has been suppressed. Either way, this message would require that things change, cascading from one precept to the next on many other customs and practices of the Church. If the Church reframes our understanding of sin in a more compassionate and empathetic way, consider the consequences to it teachings. What about eternal punishment? Without sin, what are the consequences of wrongdoing? The Church and its clergy would need to acknowledge the complexities of human nature and the myriad factors that influence its decisions. It would need to focus on helping its congregation to navigate the complexities of life, rather than condemning them for their perceived shortcomings and threatening them with eternal punishment.

"But we all know, too, that the wheels of progress move glacially in the Vatican. I've little doubt that this profound document will be debated for years before we see any real change, if we ever do."

CHAPTER
TWELVE

Felix Bauer hailed from the picturesque town of Thun in the Canton of Bern, Switzerland. He was raised in a modest household, with his father working as a local school teacher and his mother as a baker. From a young age, Felix was imbued with a profound sense of duty and an unshakeable faith, nurtured by his parents' teachings and the comforting chimes of the Stadtkirche Thun ringing across the town every Sunday.

As a teenager, Felix displayed a keen sense of discipline and a strong desire to serve. Inspired by stories of the Pontifical Swiss Guard, he dreamt of one day joining their illustrious ranks. After completing his mandatory military service in Switzerland—an experience that fortified his discipline and strategic thinking—he set off for Rome, driven by his faith and the dream sewn into his heart.

Felix's dedication and discipline saw him successfully join the Swiss Guard. His commitment to duty and his understanding of the Church's workings quickly distinguished him, earning the respect of his peers and superiors. But his time at the Vatican was not just about service and discipline. He found himself immersed in a rich tapestry of history, faith, and politics, an experience that deepened his understanding of the Church.

As a Swiss Guard, Felix had always found comfort in his role, his duties defined and straightforward. His life was defined by the rhythm of the Vatican, the solemnity of Mass, the changing of the Guard. But beneath his dutiful exterior lay a questioning mind. He'd always been curious about the deeper workings of the Church and its stance on various issues, including the role of women within its ranks.

IN THE OPULENCE of Lord Lucius Pelham's city mansion, nestled discreetly in the heart of London, Pelham sat opposite Felix Bauer. Their surroundings echoed with a grandeur that contrasted sharply with Felix's uniformed modesty. Across from them, Cardinal Bennett Dreyfus, a man who wielded significant influence within the Vatican, presided over the meeting. His mere presence lent weight and gravity to the clandestine discussion, as everyone knew he was on the short list of *papabile*, those believed to be at the front of the line as papal candidates. Already the Cardinal had briefly outlined the theft of a questionable book from the very heart of the abbey and by none other than another of the clergy. Felix was appalled by the audacity of that act alone.

"Corporal Bauer," Pelham began, his fingers toying with the stem of his half-filled wine glass. "We find ourselves at a crucial crossroads in the history of our holy Church."

Felix's blue eyes flickered with guarded curiosity, the firelight catching the determined set of his jaw. He listened with the attentiveness bred into his very bones, his entire bearing one of respectful attention.

"Father Dominic's discovery," Dreyfus interjected, his voice smooth and steady, carrying the undeniable authority of his station, "has the potential to cause unprecedented disruption. We are talking about a tremor that could ripple through the very fabric of our faith."

"A disruption?" Felix echoed, his voice firm yet brimming with concern. The unspoken question remained— was it not the duty of the Swiss Guard to protect the Church from such disruptions?

Pelham, perceptive as ever, caught the undercurrents of Felix's thoughts. He leaned forward, his gaze locking with Felix's. "Indeed, a disruption. One that could lead to dissension, even disillusionment among our flock."

For a moment, the room fell silent, save for the distant echo of London's evening bustle. Pelham allowed the implication of his words to hang in the air, the metaphorical storm cloud they painted dark and foreboding.

"Imagine, Felix," Dreyfus continued, breaking the silence. His tone was empathetic, playing the part of a concerned shepherd. "If this preposterous diary of a supposedly female Pope Joan was to be made public, many of our devoted would struggle to reconcile their faith with the reality presented to them."

"Their belief, the cornerstone of their lives, could shatter," Pelham added, the gravity in his voice mirroring the seriousness in his gaze. "The Church, as we know it, could face a crisis of faith on a global scale."

Despite his misgivings, Felix found the seeds of doubt being planted. He was a protector of the Church, of its sanctity and stability. The picture Pelham and Dreyfus painted showed a Church on the brink of turmoil and he, unwittingly, in the midst of it.

"But we," Dreyfus pointed out, encompassing the three of them with a sweep of his hand, "have an opportunity here, to protect the Church, to ensure its continuity. You, Corporal Bauer, could play a crucial role in safeguarding our Church's future."

It was a masterful stroke, appealing to Felix's unwavering sense of duty. But it was Pelham's next words that truly stoked the embers of persuasion.

"You've dedicated your life to the service of the Church, Bauer. This is… this is a call to arms. One that goes beyond the physical protection of the Holy See. It is a call to protect the faith, the belief, the very spirit of our Church."

Felix's gaze hardened, his thoughts a tempestuous sea. Yet, in the eye of the storm, the resolute light of duty beckoned him. Duty to the Church, to the faith he held dear. As the words settled around him, Felix felt the weight of his potential role, the scale of the responsibility being entrusted to him.

He had yet to fully understand how deep this rabbit hole went, how much this would test his loyalty and his faith. He was yet to witness the lengths to which Dreyfus and Pelham would go to achieve their objectives, or to feel the stirrings of a conscience wrestling with itself. But for now, in the dimly lit room of a noble's mansion built to impress, Felix Bauer found himself drawn into the fold, into a plot that would shake his world to its core.

~

IT BEING MONDAY—AND with Michael's meeting at the British Museum set for the next morning—he decided it would be best to leave for London later that day and find a hotel for a couple of nights.

"So, who's up for a jaunt to London?" he asked.

"Count me in," Hana said, raising her hand.

"Me, too," said Aaron as he downed the last of his coffee.

Lukas glanced at Karl. "Well, that was our original plan anyway, so why not? We're in too, Father Michael."

Robbie looked at his mother, who gave him a slightly disapproving look. "I really should stay behind and help my family with estate chores while on my break," he said glumly, preferring to be part of whatever Father Michael had planned. He had come to like the young priest and wanted to soak up more of his positive energy.

"Then we can take my Jeep," Karl said. "It can hold five easily. When do we leave, Michael?"

"Oh, I'd say in an hour or so. But since Robbie isn't coming, is there any reason we need to come back to Saxon Hall, or even Sherborne Abbey? We can just head back to Rome when we're done in London. If the Dorset Police need to reach us, they have my card. I wish I'd been able to discuss what we found with Reverend Andrews, to go through proper channels, so to speak."

"Well, with the demand you got from Lord Pelham, I doubt Andrews would have been able to help you keep it for the Vatican," Hana objected.

"True," Michael said. "The real point is, they were meant to be found, period. It's not like they belong to anyone but history, in my view. And with Reverend Andrews now gone, we don't even know who to contact in his place."

"I'd be loathe to turn anything over to Lord Pelham, since he's the only other person we met there," said Hana. "I would question his jurisdiction, anyway. What a creepy man."

"Oh, he's probably not all that bad," Michael said in Pelham's defense. "Maybe he had a terrible childhood or some other mitigating factor that caused him to be so curmudgeonly. It happens, you know. Remember Cardinal Dante?"

AFTER A LEISURELY THREE-HOUR DRIVE, Michael, Hana, and Aaron arrived in the bustling city of London later that afternoon. On the way, Hana had made arrangements for them to stay at the Kimpton Fitzroy, a lovely boutique hotel in the city's Bloomsbury neighborhood, not from from the British Museum.

As he drove, Michael was mentally calculating the required time needed for his exhibition program planning so Hana could make return flight arrangements.

"I'd estimate my business here may require a couple days, but expect we can safely leave for Rome by day three. Karl said he and Lukas should have arrived back by then and they'd happily pick us up at the airport. We can coordinate with him then.

"And while I'm doing that, you and Aaron can enjoy the best of what this great city has to offer."

As Aaron glanced at Hana with a smile of anticipation, Michael's phone rang. Caller ID showed Dorset Police calling. He answered it.

"Good afternoon, Father. This is DI Dempsey here in Sherborne," the lyrical voice said. "Have you got a few minutes to speak now?"

"Of course, Inspector. How can I help?"

"Forensics was able to come up with a partial fingerprint on that medallion you found. Now, you're sure your man did not touch it himself, right?"

"That's right. Sergeant Dengler knows how to treat crime scene evidence. I watched him handle the coin with his jacket cuff, by the edges."

"Good enough, then. I should probably mention that Reverend Andrews neither took his own life nor died by natural causes, making this a murder investigation now. Do you know of anyone who might have wanted harm to come to the vicar, Father?"

"No, but then as we said in our statements, we didn't know anybody there, apart from one encounter with Reverend Andrews when we first arrived, at which time he seemed to have had an altercation with Lord Pelham. At least Pelham was being rather vocal before storming out and immediately after that we saw Reverend Andrews, so I assume that was who Lord Pelham was addressing."

"Yes, we are aware of His Lordship's... well, peppery nature. But as it happens, we interviewed him just yesterday, Father, and he said he saw *you* arguing with Reverend Andrews. Would you mind telling me what that argument was about?"

"*What?!* That's absurd! I've got five other witnesses who will confirm I never once spoke to the vicar after he greeted us that first day, since we were all together the entire time. Why would Lord Pelham say such a thing, I wonder?"

"Yes, I wondered that, too." It was clear to Michael that Dempsey might be toying with him. But to what end?

"I'm curious, Inspector. Where does that partial fingerprint figure into things?"

Dempsey paused before answering. "Well, it doesn't give us enough unique points to form a full picture, I'm afraid. But we'll still be running it against databases at Interpol and through the Schengen Information System, as well as various European countries' individual databases. That will take time, and since the print is only a partial, that makes it more difficult to match. But we'll have some candidates soon enough, I'm confident.

"In the meantime, Father, I'd be grateful if you could remain accessible to us. I'm sure we'll speak again soon, so, goodbye for now."

CHAPTER
THIRTEEN

Michael had booked a rental car for the three days they expected to be in London, and until they needed it for dinner that evening, the vehicle sat on the street outside the hotel in the shade of a weeping willow tree. Its sleek, black exterior shone in the occasional peeking of sunlight through the canopy of green overhead, a peaceful picture of anticipation for the journey it was soon to undertake.

As the day waned, a pair of men rounded the corner onto the street. They were dressed in matching gray overalls and wore caps that hid their eyes beneath the shade. A small, unmarked white van trailed behind them, an accomplice at the wheel. It was a typical sight in the city—workmen going about their business, the humdrum rhythm of everyday life.

They approached the car beneath the willow tree, one of them whistling a tune lost in the city noise. The other man, the taller one, carried a toolbox that clinked with each step. They seemed just like any other city workers, making their rounds.

But beneath the veneer of mundanity, something was amiss. A certain restlessness was palpable in their movements, a stealthy look thrown over the shoulder, an uneasy shuffling of feet. They were men on a mission, their attention fixed on the black rental car beneath the willow tree.

Without a word, they started their work. The taller man with the toolbox crouched near the car's front wheel, while the other stood watch, his gaze darting up and down the street. To a casual observer, it seemed like routine maintenance work, a pre-scheduled check-up maybe.

The taller man's gloved hands moved with practiced precision, the tools from his box glinting in the dim light. Time seemed to stretch and contract around them, the city's heartbeat fading into the background.

After what seemed like an eternity, the man rose, wiping his brow with a swift motion. He threw a nod to his companion, a silent communication exchanged. As swiftly as they arrived, they packed their tools, the toolbox closing with a soft click.

With one last, lingering glance at the car under the willow tree, they climbed into their unmarked van and drove off, merging with the city's bustling traffic. Their brief presence on the street outside the hotel disappeared as if they were never there, leaving behind just a faint echo of unease.

In the quiet that followed, the rental car sat undisturbed, its glossy exterior reflecting the fading daylight. There was nothing to suggest that anything had been tampered with, no outward sign of intrusion. But beneath the surface, the machinations of Lord Pelham's henchmen had just set a dangerous stage, an unspoken threat lying in wait.

THE CITY of London was drenched in a golden hue as the sun began its descent towards the horizon. On a recommendation from a friend, Hana had settled on The Black Swan as their restaurant for the evening, an unpretentious little place just southwest of the city with a fine international menu.

Michael sat hunched over the steering wheel, his gaze fixed ahead with determination as the rental car moved like a swift shadow on the M25 motorway, cutting through the waves of traffic with the ease of a practiced hand on the wheel. The challenge of piloting a right-hand drive car was new to him, though. It was an awkward dance of untrained muscle memory and intense focus, but he managed.

Hana sat beside him, her fingers absently flipping through a road map. Aaron, in the back seat, was lost in thought, his eyes absently taking in the rapidly passing cityscape.

The rhythm of the road under the tires was like a well-orchestrated symphony, harmonious in its predictability. Then, a discordant note. Michael's foot pressed lightly on the brake, intending to adjust their speed in the ebb and flow of the traffic. The brake pedal went down with ease, but the car didn't respond. He frowned, an icy chill creeping up his spine, and pushed harder. Again, the car continued its relentless pace, heedless of his command.

"Guys," he voiced out calmly, trying to mask the

sudden surge of adrenaline, "we've got a situation here."

A glance from Hana, eyes wide with alarm, "What's wrong?"

"The brakes," he said, his voice grim, pressing the pedal to the floor to demonstrate. "They're not responding. And the accelerator is stuck!"

A gasp escaped Hana's lips, her fingers tightening around the map. In the rearview mirror, Michael saw Aaron's eyes widen in shock. The peaceful drive had taken a sharp turn into a nightmare, and they were barreling down a motorway in an unstoppable car.

But panic wasn't an option. Michael drew a deep breath, wrestling his fear into submission with a quick prayer. He downshifted, hoping the engine could slow them a bit. But the high-speed momentum defied his efforts, the car continuing its terrifyingly unchecked roll forward.

Ahead, the motorway curved like a sinuous beast, and Michael guided the car with meticulous precision. He swerved around a heavy goods truck, the tires screaming with protest against the sudden change. The noise from honking cars filled the air like an orchestra of doom, their drivers' faces flashing by, contorted with fear and anger.

"Find a safe exit!" Michael commanded Hana, his knuckles turning white against the dark steering wheel. She nodded, her gaze scanning the fast-approaching exits and overpasses.

"There's one… about a mile up ahead," she informed, her voice trembling with trepidation but maintaining a semblance of control.

Their journey turned into a high-speed slalom, swerving in and out of lanes, narrowly avoiding collisions, hearts hammering in unison. Every maneuver, every calculated risk was a dance with danger, each move leaving them teetering on the precipice of disaster.

"Try the handbrake!" Aaron's voice sliced through the cacophony from the backseat.

Michael glanced at the rapidly approaching exit. "On my count. We don't want to flip," he warned.

With a final turn of the wheel, they were bearing down on the exit. Michael took a deep breath, counting down, "Three… two… one…" Then he pulled the handbrake. The car lurched, the tires let out a soul-curdling scream, and for a brief, terrifying moment, the car swayed precariously between control and chaos.

But Michael was not about to let chaos win. With an iron grip and sheer will, he kept the car in line, steering it off the motorway. The wind from the slightly opened window howled in his ears, and the world outside was a blur of colors as they took the exit.

Ahead, Hana pointed out a gravelly lay-by at the side of the road. "There! Aim for there," she directed.

Michael's eyes focused on the lay-by, a mere speck in the distance growing rapidly larger as they hurtled towards it. "Brace yourselves," he warned, veering the car onto the rough terrain.

The tires hit the gravel, skidding and spewing up a plume of dust. The car fishtailed wildly, the back end swerving from side to side, threatening to throw them into a deathly spin. But with every skid, Michael counter-steered, struggling to get the vehicle back into a straight line. Even throwing the gearshift into Neutral failed to work; it functioned the same as the Drive gear.

The world outside was a blur of dust and fear, each second stretching into a minute, every minute an eternity. But gradually, their speed started to reduce. The momentum they had been slaves to was finally losing its grip on them.

Every muscle in Michael's body strained as he continued to fight the wheel. Their speed had dropped significantly, but the car was still lurching erratically. He needed to get it under control. With a final burst of determination, he wrestled the vehicle into a straight path.

The sound of the crunching gravel under the car slowly dimmed, replaced by the loud thumps of their hearts. Finally, the car stuttered to a halt. An eerie silence descended, the echo of their wild ride seeming to reverberate in the air around them.

For a moment, they all sat still, their breathing heavy and ragged, the adrenaline still coursing through their veins. The only other sound was the ticking of the engine as it began to cool.

"We're... we're alive," Hana breathed out in disbelief, her voice shaking. Michael loosened his grip on the steering wheel, his knuckles aching. He glanced at Aaron in the rearview mirror, their eyes meeting in a silent acknowledgment of the unspoken threat that still loomed over them.

"Is anyone else thinking what I'm thinking?" Hana asked. "That this was no accident?"

"But who would want to cause us harm?" Aaron asked in a high-pitched voice, protesting the very thought. "What have we done to deserve this?"

"It may be what we haven't done," Michael said. "And Lucius Pelham comes to mind in that sense. He as much as threatened me on the phone before we left Robbie's, though this seems a rather extreme way to demonstrate his displeasure."

If so, the emerging shadow of Lord Pelham had just turned even more sinister. And for some reason, Michael felt this was only the beginning.

BACK IN HIS hotel room after arranging for a new rental car, then finally having dinner, Michael was seated alone by the window, meditating on events of the evening, when the shrill ring of the room telephone shattered his peaceful reverie. With a sigh, he rose from the velvet armchair and picked up the receiver.

"This is Michael Dominic."

"Good evening, Father Dominic," came a warm, Italian-accented voice. "My name is Brother Lando Spinosa. I am calling from the Monastery of Santa Maria di Grottaferrata, up in the hills just outside of Rome, calling on behalf of the Fellowship of the True Faith. Are you aware of our organization?"

"Brother Spinosa..." Michael repeated, his brows furrowing. "I'm afraid I'm unfamiliar with you or your Fellowship."

"That is as it should be," Brother Spinosa began, his tone earnest, "as our very existence is a carefully guarded secret. I suggest you ask His Holiness about our bona fides; he is one of the few in the Vatican with such knowledge. I understand this is unexpected, and perhaps even odd, but we have a situation here, one we think you could help with."

"And what would that be?" Michael asked, his curiosity piqued despite his initial wariness.

"It involves Lord Lucius Pelham, head of the Order of Papal Guardians, and someone I understand you are familiar with. It appears—or so we are told—that Lord Pelham is intent on acquiring the Pope Joan diary in your possession, and his methods, I'm afraid, are far from ethical," Spinosa said, a note of concern coloring his voice.

Thinking back to the evening's earlier events, a chill went down Michael's spine as he processed the information. "I see. Well, you certainly are informed, as very few people even know about this diary. And yes, I am quite familiar with Lord Pelham's pursuits—more than I'd like to be, frankly—but, how did you know how to reach me, much less what I might have in my possession?"

The line was quiet for a moment before Brother Spinosa replied. "Our paths have been guided to intersect, Father. I know it may seem unusual, but we have mutual friends who vouched for you and have been watching out for you from a distance. They said you would understand the implications of this situation."

"And you're hoping I can help, is that it?"

"Precisely," Spinosa affirmed. "We would like to invite you to a confidential meeting at our monastery when you return to Rome. We need your wisdom and guidance to counter Lord Pelham's unholy efforts and preserve Pope Joan's diary."

Michael was intrigued. After a moment, he responded, "As it turns out, I'll be back in Rome in a few days. I will be able to meet with you then."

Brother Spinosa's relief was palpable. "Thank you, Father Dominic. We look forward to seeing you. I hope together we can stop this man's devilish intentions."

After exchanging contact information, they ended the call. Outside, the city of London pulsed with life, oblivious to the shadowy ballet of power and conspiracy extending across nations and organizations.

CHAPTER

FOURTEEN

After an early breakfast the next morning, Michael and Hana were seated in the quiet solitude of the hotel's library, their discoveries in Sherborne Abbey laying on the table between them: the worn diary of Pope Joan and the parchment page of the Gospel of St. Salome.

"Pope Joan was, undeniably, a remarkable woman," Michael began, his voice echoing softly against walls lined with a warm mauve moire fabric. "But her existence and beliefs challenge the very fundamentals of the Church's structure."

Hana nodded thoughtfully, her fingers tracing the edge of Pope Joan's diary. "Yes, and the repercussions could be vast. The idea that a woman once led the Church, that she achieved such a position while disguised as a man... It could shake the Church to its core."

She hesitated, looking up at Michael. "But it's not just the fact of her existence, it's her views on the role of women within the Church. If her perspectives were to come to light—not to mention her obscured legitimacy as pope—there could be calls for dramatic shifts in doctrine and practice."

Michael leaned back in his chair, his mind racing with the implications. "We are living in modern times, Hana. There is a growing demand for gender equality, even within the Church. Perhaps Pope Ignatius will see this as an opportunity to address these demands. But it won't be easy. There will be resistance, dissent."

Hana interjected, "And what about the Gospel of St. Salome? Her views on sin alone and its use as a control mechanism are revolutionary, potentially subversive."

"Indeed," Michael acknowledged, picking up the ancient document. "Her Gospel presents a perspective that could challenge centuries of teachings about sin and repentance. It is an even greater point of tension the pope will need to navigate."

They sat in silence for a moment, the magnitude of their task ahead settling heavily.

"Do you think Pope Ignatius is ready for this?" Hana finally asked.

"He's a wise and compassionate leader," Michael replied after a moment's thought. "He has always shown a willingness to adapt and evolve. But this… these revelations are seismic. They have the power to completely reshape the Church as we know it."

"But isn't that precisely what the Church might need?" Hana pressed. "A shake-up, a radical re-evaluation of its doctrines and practices?"

Michael looked at her for a long moment. "Yes, perhaps it is. But change, especially on such a scale, is difficult. And it's not without risks. The Holy Father could choose to embrace these revelations, to use them as a catalyst for change. He could call for more inclusivity in the Church, a redefinition of sin, and a shift in power dynamics. But such changes could also cause a rift within the Church, with traditionalists resisting and progressives pushing for even more change.

"And there's another path," Michael went on, his gaze falling on Pope Joan's diary. "The pope could also decide to keep these revelations a secret, to protect the Church and its believers from the turmoil they would undoubtedly cause. But that too has its risks. If the truth were to leak, the Church could be seen as withholding critical information, causing further distrust. Frankly, it could also lead to a schism. To resistance, anger, even violence. Are we ready to face that? How will the pope choose to navigate this path, especially given his current state of health?"

He looked at Hana, her gaze fixed on the ancient documents before them. "All we can do now is present him with these revelations and support him as he makes these difficult decisions."

Their conversation echoed softly within the quiet library, a prelude to the monumental discussions that were about to take place when they returned to Rome. Whatever happened next, it could well be that the Church was on the brink of profound change.

ONCE AARON HAD AWAKENED, showered, and had a bit of breakfast, he and Hana decided to walk the streets around the hotel while Michael left for the British

Museum and his final planning sessions with the curator there for the approaching exhibition.

Aaron and Hana soon found themselves meandering through the rain-kissed streets of Bloomsbury, their breath misting in the cool London morning. Their surroundings were beautiful in their historical charm, but it was clear their minds were preoccupied with a shared, unspoken tension.

Aaron was the first to break the silence, his voice echoing softly in the quiet street. "Hana, though we haven't known each other all that long, our friendship has been built on transparency and trust. And I think it's time we address the elephant in the room."

Hana turned her face to him, her brows furrowed in puzzlement, but with a hint of understanding in her eyes. "Of course, Aaron. What's on your mind?"

Aaron took a deep breath, steadying his nerves before he said, "It's about Michael. You two share a special connection, I think. It's deeper than mere friendship, isn't it?"

There was a moment's silence as Hana processed Aaron's words. Her face, normally so expressive, betrayed little. But there was a flicker in her eyes, a momentary shadow that confirmed what Aaron suspected.

"Hana…" Aaron began, but she interjected.

"Aaron, I… what are you suggesting?" she asked, her voice almost a whisper.

Aaron stopped in his tracks, his gaze steady as he met Hana's. "Hana, I care for you, deeply. And Michael is my best friend. But it's clear there is… something unspoken between you two. Something that's more than friend-ship. I've seen the way you look at each other, the way you interact. It's as if there's a private language between the two of you."

The silence was palpable as Hana looked away, her gaze distant. Aaron could see her wrestling with her thoughts. Finally, she met his eyes, "Aaron, your observation isn't entirely off the mark," she admitted, her voice barely a whisper. "Yes, there is something between us. But we've never really addressed it. Never given voice to it. Never truly acted on it. He's a priest, and I… well, it's complicated."

Aaron nodded, understanding and sympathy washing over him. "And yet, here we are. You and me. We're kind of dating."

"Yes," Hana admitted, a rueful chuckle escaping her lips. "Yes, we are. It's not a simple situation, is it?"

Aaron reached out and gently took her hand. She didn't pull away, but looked at him with a mixture of surprise and gratitude. "Hana, it's only a predicament if we make it one," he said. "We all have a history. We all have unspoken feelings and complexities. What's important is that we're honest with each other, with ourselves."

Hana looked at him, her eyes reflecting a storm of emotions—appreciation, guilt, and a hint of regret. "Aaron, you're a remarkable man. Your understanding and honesty… it's humbling. But I don't know what the next step is."

Aaron squeezed her hand reassuringly, "Maybe it's not about finding a solution," he suggested. "Maybe it's simply about acceptance. About understanding and coming to terms with these feelings. We could start by being open about this with Michael. We owe him that."

Hana sighed, her eyes glinting with unshed tears, "You make it sound so uncomplicated, Aaron."

Shrugging, he offered her a gentle smile. "Well, it's definitely not uncomplicated," he admitted. "But we can handle this. We're adults, after all. And what's important is that we handle it with candor and virtue."

With a tremulous smile, Hana nodded. "Thank you, Aaron. For being patient, and understanding, and... well, so damn honorable."

Aaron pulled her into a gentle hug, whispering, "Always, Hana. Always."

Their conversation, heartfelt and earnest, reverberated around them as they resumed their walk. They were threading their way through a maze of emotions and complex feelings. But they were not lost; instead, they were stepping forward, embracing their honesty, walking towards a future that was uncertain, but faced with integrity.

CHAPTER
FIFTEEN

Father Michael and Skyler Armitage sat across from each other in the curator's office at the British Museum, surrounded by maps and artifact lists strewn over the desk.

"Father Dominic, it's good to finally meet in person," Skyler began, extending a hand across the desk. Michael shook it warmly, his smile sincere.

"Likewise, Skyler. This joint venture is a remarkable endeavor. I'm excited to see it all come together."

Skyler nodded, spreading his hands over the diagrams before them. "We have a unique opportunity here, to bring these pieces of history from both the British Museum and Vatican Apostolic Archives together… it's an undertaking, to be sure, but one we are enthusiastic about."

Michael's gaze scanned over the layouts of the various departments that would be used in the exhibition. "I believe *Echoes of Faith* can create an immersive journey through the Church's history for the visitors.

Each artifact carries with it a story, a whisper of the past, don't you agree?"

"Absolutely," Skyler agreed, his face lighting up with the passion he held for his work. "I've always believed that each object in our care holds a piece of our shared human story. And to provide people a glimpse into the past through these artifacts is a responsibility we curators do not take lightly."

A mutual excitement filled the room as they discussed the exhibit. It wasn't just about presenting historical artifacts. It was about weaving the individual threads of history into a rich tapestry, providing a shared space for faith and history in the hearts of their visitors.

As Michael had predicted, it took the better part of two full days of final planning at the British Museum for the upcoming exhibition.

Over the past year Michael and his team at the Apostolic Archives had been working with Skyler Armitage, the museum's curator for the Britain, Europe and Prehistory Department, and could see that he might be spending more time in London in the coming days as the exhibition was just two weeks away.

It would be a day of unprecedented collaboration, a day that would etch itself deeply into the annals of history. The British Museum and the Vatican Apostolic Archives, two monumental institutions of culture and knowledge, had come together to organize an exhibit like no other. This was not merely an exhibition—it was a spiritual journey, a leap across centuries of devotion, a vivid communion with the past.

The title of the exhibition, *Echoes of Faith: A Joint Retrospective of Church Artifacts*, sought to unravel the enigmatic layers of history, offering a panoramic view of the

Church's role as a bearer of faith and a catalyst for art, culture, and civilization. From the moment visitors stepped into the grand foyer of the British Museum, they would be enveloped by a profound sense of reverence and awe, the air resonating with the silent whispers of yesteryears.

The first section of the exhibition was *The Scribes of God: Manuscripts and Documents*. Here, the Vatican had granted the public a rare glimpse into its Apostolic Archives. The display included a breathtaking array of manuscripts, some dating back to the early centuries of the Christian Era. The Codex Vaticanus, one of the oldest known copies of the Greek Bible, was a centerpiece. Its delicate, faded pages were a testament to the countless hands that had held it, the innumerable voices that had read it aloud.

Next, it was the *Relics: Tangible Echoes of Saints*. In a carefully climate-controlled environment, a collection of precious reliquaries glowed dimly. The Shard of the True Cross, a sliver of wood believed to have been part of the cross on which Jesus was crucified, stirred a sense of sacredness in the air. A thorn, purportedly from the Crown of Thorns, was enclosed in a bejeweled box of gold and glass, radiating a solemn beauty.

Following this, visitors would encounter *Vestments and Liturgical Objects*. This section showcased the intricate craftsmanship involved in the creation of ecclesiastical garments and liturgical items. A papal tiara, worn by popes of the past during coronations, gleamed under the soft lighting. Its triple tiered design shimmered with precious gemstones, a symbol of the temporal and spiritual power of the papacy. A chalice and paten, used in the celebration of the Eucharist, stood resplendent in their delicate gold-work, still echoing with the sacred words they had once accompanied.

The Art of Devotion: Sacred Art and Sculpture was a mesmerizing display of religious artistry. It housed pieces from different religious movements, including Romanesque, Gothic, Renaissance, and Baroque. The pièce de résistance was an exquisite sculpture of the Pieta, a stunning depiction of the Virgin Mary cradling the lifeless body of Christ, its marble surface seeming to pulse with raw emotion.

The final section, *Papal Histories: A Walk Through Papal Eras*, was a chronological journey through the lives and times of significant popes. Ancient letters, seals, papal bulls, and even personal effects painted a vivid picture of their reigns. Among them, a pair of worn-out slippers that once belonged to Pope John XXIII silently spoke volumes about his simplicity and dedication.

Walking through the exhibition, visitors would feel as though they had transcended time and space, stepping into the profound world of the early Church and its evolution over the centuries. The air was rich with history, the walls echoing with the hallowed prayers of those long past.

The British Museum and the Vatican Apostolic Archives had not merely organized an exhibition—they had orchestrated a sensory symphony of history, faith, and art. They allowed reflections of centuries-old devotion to resonate within modern hearts, creating a sacred space where past and present intertwined, where tangible artifacts bore witness to an intangible legacy of faith. Each artifact was not just an object—it was a narrative, a story of faith that had weathered the sands of time and continued to inspire. Even before its official opening,

Vatican and museum personnel setting up the exhibits felt how *Echoes of Faith* resonated in them long after they had left the hallowed halls of the exhibition each day, lingering in hearts and minds, a timeless testament to the power and beauty of belief.

At the end of the second day, Michael concluded his work with a visit to Skyler's office. "I'm heading back to Rome tomorrow," Michael said, "but you know how to reach me if I can help further. You've done a fantastic job here, Skyler. Our treasures couldn't be in better hands."

CHAPTER
SIXTEEN

The hum of the airplane's engines served as a soothing soundtrack to the hushed conversation in the main cabin. The flight from London to Rome had begun smoothly, and now, high above the clouds, Michael, Hana, and Aaron found themselves in reflective conversation, interspersed with bouts of quiet anticipation. Michael, cradling the diary of Pope Joan and the Gospel of St. Salome in the carry-on bag on his lap, felt the weight of the journey that had brought them to this moment.

He turned to his companions, the excitement in his voice barely concealed. "I can't wait to share these with Pope Ignatius," he admitted, gently tracing his fingers along the carry-on's seams. "They are more than historical artifacts; they represent major shifts in our understanding of Church history."

"I keep thinking back to Lord Pelham," Hana said. "What were his motivations, I wonder?"

Michael nodded, grimacing at the memory of the

phone call with the determined noble and his later lies about Michael having an argument with Father Andrews. "Yes, his motivations seemed deeply personal, maybe driven by a fear of the unknown, or perhaps of a history he didn't want to confront. Based on his call the other day, I have a suspicion he knows full and well what it is we have, and he seemed pretty desperate getting control of it. Knowing what we now know, one wonders if that's simply an issue of envious possession, or if he just doesn't want the contents known by anyone else."

There was a moment of silence, each absorbed in their own recollections. It was Hana who broke the silence, her voice soft, "Then there's Reverend Andrews..." The sentence trailed off, the ending left unspoken but understood. Reverend Andrews' death had cast a dark shadow over their expedition.

"Yes," Michael sighed, his eyes clouded with remembrance. "His death is a mystery that DI Dempsey has yet to solve. A piece of the puzzle still missing. But maybe we owe it to him to share these discoveries. Given his stewardship of the abbey, one could say he was as much a part of this journey as we are."

The plane shook slightly as it passed through a pocket of turbulence, and the seatbelt sign above flickered on. It was a sobering reminder of their current situation, thousands of feet above the ground, en route to Rome, carrying with them discoveries that could send ripples through the ecclesiastical world.

The conversation then took a lighter turn when Aaron, ever the one to find humor in the darkest of times, recalled their vehicular misadventure. "You'd think that the brakes choosing to give out after everything we'd been through would be the least of our problems."

Though it terrified them in the moment, they could laugh about it now, a welcome respite from the tension of their earlier discussion. The memory of fear replaced with the humor of hindsight.

"But here we are," Michael said once the light laughter had subsided, pointing to his carry-on satchel. His gaze was intent, serious. "Despite everything—the threats, the mystery, the dangers—we have two extraordinary artifacts each with its own penetrating content."

The cabin lights flickered, the seatbelt sign illuminating with a soft ding. They were nearing their destination. Their journey, which began in the historic depths of Sherborne Abbey and was filled with the shadowy resistance of Lord Pelham, the enigmatic death of Reverend Andrews, and a touch of vehicular terror, was drawing to a momentous conclusion.

As the plane began its descent, they all sat back, the atmosphere around them brimming with anticipation. They were returning home, not as they had left, but as torchbearers of a secret that could change the world. And as the city appeared below them, a sprawl of ancient history bathed in the long shadows of the late afternoon's light, they knew they were on the brink of an unprecedented revelation.

∼

THE SUN WAS JUST SETTING over Rome as Karl, at the wheel of his Jeep Wrangler with Lukas riding shotgun and Michael and Hana chatting in the back seat, drove toward the Vatican from Leonardo da Vinci Airport, having picked up Michael and Hana on their return from London. Going in the opposite direction, Aaron elected to take a taxi back to his apartment.

The Eternal City was awash in a resplendent golden hue, creating a serene atmosphere that belied the urgency of their mission. Michael was eager to share with Pope Ignatius the critical information he'd discovered in England.

As the car navigated the narrow, cobblestoned streets, a red VW sedan with blackout windows appeared in the rearview mirror, accelerating rapidly and closing the distance between them. Karl, an experienced driver, sensed that something was amiss and instinctively tightened his grip on the wheel. Before he could warn the others, a deafening gunshot shattered the quiet evening air, and a bullet whizzed past the car, missing it by mere inches but striking the roof of the car ahead of them.

Karl's instincts kicked into high gear, and he floored the accelerator, swerving to the left to evade the pursuing vehicle. "Hold on, everyone!" he shouted over the roaring engine, his knuckles white with tension. Lukas, equally alert, reached for his sidearm, looking back at the pursuers, ready to defend his companions.

The streets of Rome became a blur as the chase intensified. Karl expertly navigated the labyrinthine roadways, taking sharp turns and weaving through traffic with a mixture of skill and desperation. The red VW clung to their tail, relentless in its pursuit, its unseen occupants continuing to fire at the fleeing car.

Michael and Hana exchanged panicked glances in the backseat, their hearts pounding in their chests as their minds returned to London and the inconceivable similarity of losing their brakes on the M25 motorway. They knew that Pope Joan's diary and the Gospel of St. Salome might be volatile, but they hadn't expected attacks over them. *Is that what was happening?!* Michael tightened his grip on the precious artifacts, determined to protect them at all costs.

The chase led them past some of Rome's most iconic landmarks, their beauty and significance overshadowed by the life-or-death struggle unfolding around them. As Karl sped past the Colosseum, he spotted a narrow alleyway up ahead and made a split-second decision to veer into it. The red sedan followed, its tires squealing as it navigated the tight turn.

With sudden dismay, Karl's heart raced as he realized that the alleyway was a dead end. Thinking quickly, he slammed on the brakes, throwing the car into reverse and accelerating backward. The VW, caught off guard by the sudden maneuver, crashed into a pile of trash cans, momentarily disabling it.

Seizing the opportunity, Karl steered the car back around the sedan and onto the main road and accelerated once more, hoping to put some distance between them and their assailants. Lukas leaned out the window, his gun at the ready, prepared to return fire if necessary.

As they sped through the bustling Piazza Navona, narrowly avoiding pedestrians and street vendors, Lukas caught a closer look at the red sedan in his side mirror. *Curious,* he thought. *That looks a lot like... no, it couldn't be.* Realizing that their enemies may be closer than they thought, Lukas kept the information to himself, for now.

With the red sedan hot on their tail once again, Karl led the chase toward the Tiber River, his eyes scanning the environment for any opportunity to escape. As they approached the Ponte Sant'Angelo, he made a daring decision: with a sharp turn, he veered onto the pedestrian walkway of the historic bridge, barely squeezing the car between the ornate statues that lined the path.

The red sedan followed suit, its tires peeling as it navigated the narrow passage. Pedestrians scattered in terror, diving out of the way of the speeding vehicles. The chase continued along the Tiber, both cars racing at breakneck speeds, their engines roaring as they were pushed to their limits.

The majestic Castel Sant'Angelo loomed in the distance, a symbol of the Vatican's proximity and the hope of sanctuary. Karl knew that if they could reach the safety of the Vatican, they might stand a chance against their pursuers.

With renewed determination, he floored the accelerator, weaving through the increasingly dense traffic as they approached the Ponte Vittorio Emanuele II. As they crossed the bridge, Karl spotted a small side street that led in the direction of the Vatican. He took the turn at full speed, the tires protesting loudly as the car careened around the corner. The VW followed suit, its occupants unwilling to give up their pursuit.

The streets grew narrower as they neared the Vatican, the ancient buildings casting long shadows across their path. The chase continued at a breakneck pace, both cars weaving in and out of the tight confines with inches to spare.

Suddenly, the familiar sight of St. Peter's Square came into view, its expansive piazza offering a brief respite from the claustrophobic streets. Karl gunned the engine one last time, propelling the car toward the safety of St. Anne's Gate.

As they approached the entrance, the Swiss Guards on duty, recognizing Karl's Jeep, sprang into action and quickly raised the boom barrier. Karl brought the car to a screeching halt just inside the Vatican's perimeter as the VW flew past the entrance, not to be seen again.

Safe within the walls of the Vatican, the group took a moment to catch their breath, their hearts still racing from the adrenaline-fueled chase.

Lukas whispered to Karl, "I can't be sure, but I think I recognized someone in that car. He looked an awful lot like Felix Bauer. But it *couldn't* be, could it?"

Karl was surprised by Lukas' statement, but he trusted his partner's observations. "That can't be right, Lukas. Why would Corporal Bauer be after *us*?"

"What I can't believe," Hana said with some measure of anger, "is the fact that we are being targeted by someone for either or both of these artifacts you have, Michael. If Lord Pelham is behind this, we've got to alert the authorities!"

"I doubt Detective Inspector Dempsey would take action based just on two isolated attacks in two countries without stronger evidence," Karl said. "But it might help point the spotlight on him."

As they stepped out of the car and made their way toward the Apostolic Palace, Michael couldn't help but marvel at the incredible turn of events that had brought them to this point.

But he also knew that the road ahead would be fraught with challenges, and now assumed that the Order of Papal Guardians would stop at nothing to see their objectives through, whatever those might be.

CHAPTER
SEVENTEEN

M ichael Dominic and Hana Sinclair ascended the wide marble staircase leading to the pope's private apartments in the Vatican Apostolic Palace. Their steps echoed softly through the grand hallway, harmonizing with the whispers of a history that spanned two millennia. Clutched carefully in Michael's hands were two objects that had the potential to alter the course of that history: the diary of Pope Joan and the Gospel of St. Salome.

"Are you sure it's all right that I come in with you, Michael?" Hana asked, a little nervous as she contemplated being in the pope's private apartment for the first time.

"Absolutely. I've already cleared it with my father's secretary, Nick Bannon. His Holiness is looking forward to seeing you. Besides, you're as involved in this as I am."

As they approached the entrance, a Swiss Guard snapped to attention, gave them a curt nod, then stepped aside to allow them entry. Entering the private quarters of Pope Ignatius, they were enveloped in the hallowed silence, the tranquility of a space seeped in contemplation and prayer. The lingering, tranquil scent of Somalian frankincense hung in the still air.

Pope Ignatius, a figure of quiet dignity, eagerly awaited his son's arrival as he lay in his bed. He knew he had little time left, for age had been taking its toll on him for some time now. A gentle smile graced his face, the eyes reflecting a wisdom earned from years of service to the Church. "Hello, Michael. And dear Ms. Sinclair," he smiled. "I must say, it is good seeing both of you. I trust you bring news from England?"

They both smiled in return, though there was a certain resolve on Michael's face. "Your Holiness," he acknowledged before placing the precious artifacts on the table. The pope's eyes widened a fraction at the sight of the well-aged documents, recognition of something momentous flickering in his gaze.

"How to begin...? These, Holy Father, are a powerful testament to a hidden past," Michael began, gesturing towards the diary and gospel. "A past that was unearthed at Sherborne Abbey in England. A past that could reshape our understanding of the Church's history."

Pope Ignatius, his interest piqued, looked at Michael with curiosity. "Tell me more, my son."

"Well, I must first say that we've had our share of trials bringing these to light," Michael confessed, glancing at Hana. His mind filled with images of Lord Pelham, an adversary in their path to discovery, and the body of Reverend Andrews. "The road has been rife with obstacles, but here we are. In my hands, a most special diary we will get to in a moment. But here," he gestured to the second document, "is the Gospel of St. Salome, a narrative that could redefine our understanding of sin."

Pope Ignatius looked at the worn gambeson cover of the Gospel, astonishment clear on his face. "St. Salome," he murmured, the name hanging in the air as he considered it. "I never thought I'd see something written by her hand. She is a somewhat overlooked figure in our gospels."

His gaze shifted from the document to both of his guests, a glint of curiosity in his eyes. "Salome, if my memory serves me right, was a follower of Jesus, present at both his crucifixion and resurrection. Some say that she was the mother of the apostles James and John, and is often believed to be a sister of Mary, the mother of Jesus. A woman of faith and strength. Isn't that so, Michael?"

Michael nodded, affirming the pope's memory, then turned his gaze back to the document, his fingers gently touching the weathered surface. The pope's words seemed to drift in the room, floating alongside the dust motes caught in the shafts of afternoon sunlight. The Gospel of St. Salome, a testament from the hand of a woman of faith, was a fragment of the past that held the potential to resonate into the future of the Church.

The air in the room was heavy with centuries of whispered prayers and the weight of Church history. Now, picking up the diary, Michael held a piece of that history in his hands, a story long discredited and pushed to the edges of Church lore—the diary of Pope Joan.

"Your Holiness," he began, his voice reverberating in the grand chamber. "What I have here," he motioned to the book he had laid on the table, "could fundamentally reshape our understanding of the Church's history."

Pope Ignatius looked at him intently. "And what would that be, Michael?"

The young priest paused, his eyes glancing down at the aged parchment pages of the journal. "This is the diary of Pope Joan," he stated, meeting the pope's gaze.

Pope Ignatius looked at him in astonishment. "Pope Joan? You can't be serious! The mythical female pope from the Middle Ages? That's a story, Michael, nothing more than legend."

"Or so we've been led to believe, Papa. But legend or not, this diary claims otherwise, and convincingly so," Michael said as he carefully opened the book's worn pages. "The text within is written in Old Anglo-Saxon English, and it details her life, her ascension, her pontificate, and the immense struggle she faced hiding her true identity."

Pope Ignatius looked contemplative, "But the Church has always taught that only baptized males can be ordained... This goes against tradition and doctrine."

"But does it really defy the teachings of Christ, Your Holiness?" Michael asked gently. "Remember Galatians 3:28: *'There is neither Jew nor Gentile, neither slave nor free, nor is there male and female, for you are all one in Christ Jesus.'* Should we not contemplate this in light of our new discoveries?"

For a moment, silence filled the room as Pope Ignatius absorbed the implications. "And if this is indeed true, Michael," he asked, "what impact do you foresee on the Church?"

Michael took a deep breath. "We've always held that the Church was solely led by men. This could challenge that belief system, but it could also open a door… a door to greater inclusion."

"Inclusion?" the pope repeated, his brow furrowed.

"Women, Your Holiness," Michael replied. "This diary doesn't merely tell the tale of Pope Joan. It's a testament to her courage, her wisdom, and her faith. She led the Church at a time when women had little say in matters of religion, let alone be in a position of leadership."

Pope Ignatius leaned back in his bed, his gaze contemplative. "It's a radical idea, Michael. Many within the Church will resist such a change."

"But change is often the result of truth, Your Holiness," Michael countered gently. "This truth has presented itself, and it's our duty to confront and understand it. If Pope Joan's legitimacy comes to light, it could inspire us to reevaluate women's roles within the Church. Perhaps it's time we let women have a more significant influence, not because of Pope Joan, but because they represent half of the Church's body. Their insights, perspectives, and leadership could only enrich us."

Pope Ignatius was silent for a long time. Michael watched him, knowing he had given the man much to consider.

"Courage, wisdom, faith…" Pope Ignatius finally murmured, seemingly more to himself than to Michael, "These virtues are not limited by gender, are they?"

"No, they aren't, Your Holiness," Michael confirmed.

With a sigh, the pope resettled himself in the bed, a man bearing the weight of the world on his shoulders. "We preach love, understanding, and inclusion, don't we, Michael?" he said, looking out of the window at the heart of Vatican City. "Perhaps it is time we practice it fully within our own walls as well. I must give this more thought. A great deal more."

"And as for this Gospel of St. Salome," Michael enthused, "well, the very fact of its having survived two thousand years and remains one of the only artifacts we have from an actual disciple of Jesus while he was living —that alone is breathtaking in itself. But wait until you hear what she writes about, Papa."

Michael took another deep breath and began reading the gospel to the Holy Father. When he was finished, he looked into his father's eyes.

"Throughout the centuries, the Church has wielded considerable power and influence over the lives of the faithful. One of the primary ways this has been achieved is through the concept of 'sin.' And to be perfectly honest, sin has long been used as a means to control and direct the actions and beliefs of the masses.

"However," he continued, "the world is changing, and so too must the Church. It is becoming increasingly apparent that the concept of sin is losing its potency as a tool for maintaining control over the faithful. We must recognize this shift and adapt our teachings accordingly, lest we risk losing our relevance and authority."

Pope Ignatius leaned forward, his interest piqued by his son's observations. "Tell me more, Michael. Why do you believe the concept of sin is no longer as effective as it once was?"

Michael considered his response, then said, "There are several factors at play. First, we live in a rapidly secu-larizing world. The influence of religious institutions is waning, and many people are seeking answers to their existential questions outside the realm of faith. They are turning to science, philosophy, and other belief systems to make sense of their lives and the world around them.

"Second," he continued, "our understanding of human nature has evolved. Modern psychology has shown us that people are not inherently evil, but rather, they are influenced by their environment and experiences. This challenges the traditional concept of sin as an innate and immutable aspect of our being.

"Your Holiness, we must reframe our understanding of sin in a more compassionate and empathetic manner. By acknowledging the complexities of human nature and the myriad factors that influence our actions, we can guide the faithful towards spiritual growth and self-reflection, rather than relying on fear and manipulation.

"Furthermore," he added, "we must shift our focus from punishment and judgment to love, compassion, and forgiveness, just as St. Salome proclaimed that Jesus had taught in the first century. We must demonstrate that the Church is here to help the faithful navigate the challenges of life, not to condemn them for their perceived shortcomings."

Pope Ignatius considered Michael's words carefully, his eyes conveying a sense of deep introspection. "In your view, then, how might we begin this transformation?"

"Well, first, Papa, I would never presume to school you on any subject, especially on such fundamental matters of faith. But since you asked for my opinion, please take it for what it's worth, as I've given this some thought since discovering St. Salome's Gospel.

"We can start," the young priest continued, "by engaging in open and honest conversations with our clergy and laity about the changing role of sin in our faith. We must listen to their concerns, questions, and doubts, addressing them with understanding and empathy.

"Next, we must reevaluate our catechism, homilies, and pastoral care to ensure that our message is aligned with this new understanding of sin. We should emphasize spiritual growth, self-reflection, and the importance of forgiveness, rather than dwelling on the fear of divine retribution."

Pope Ignatius looked thoughtfully at Michael, weighing the significant implications of his words. He took a deep breath before responding, his voice calm yet firm.

"Michael, I understand and appreciate the passion you bring to this issue. Indeed, the Church must always be open to change and growth. However, we must also recognize that the traditional concept of sin is deeply enmeshed in the very fabric of our faith. It has been a cornerstone of our teachings and practices for centuries, and any attempt to reverse this would be a monumental undertaking, perhaps taking generations to accomplish."

Michael listened intently, the heft of the pope's words not lost on him.

The Holy Father continued, "Reflecting on the words of Salome, they have provided us with a unique perspective on the teachings of Christ, and it certainly gives me much to consider. Yet we have the other gospels to still consider as well. We must be cautious, therefore, in how we proceed.

"The faithful have long relied on the Church's teachings and guidance in their spiritual journeys. The concept of sin, as it has been traditionally taught, has provided a moral compass for countless generations. To

suddenly shift our understanding of sin would undoubtedly create confusion and turmoil among the faithful,
potentially leading to a loss of trust in the Church's
authority."

Michael hesitated before responding. "Holy Father, I
understand your concerns. However, I believe that we
must find a way to strike a balance between preserving
the core of our faith and adapting to the evolving world
around us. If we remain steadfast in our traditional
teachings, we risk losing touch with the very people we
are meant to guide."

Pope Ignatius nodded, his expression thoughtful. "I
agree, Michael, that we must adapt and grow. But we
must do so with great care and discernment. We cannot
simply cast aside centuries of tradition overnight and on
the weight of only one gospel. We must carefully
consider the consequences of such a drastic shift in our
teachings, and ensure that we are not causing more harm
than good.

"Your insights and dedication to this matter are
invaluable, my son. I trust that eventually we can navigate the equilibrium between tradition and progress. We
must work diligently to understand the needs and
concerns of the faithful, while also acknowledging and
honoring the rich history and tradition that has shaped
our faith."

Pope Ignatius, gently handling the diary of Pope
Joan, looked up at Hana, whose curiosity was apparent
in her attentive gaze. "Ms. Sinclair," he began, acknowledging her vital role in the discovery, "as a journalist,
your profession thrives on truth and disclosure. You
unravel stories for the world, a task not too dissimilar to
what we are attempting here."

The pope laid the diary down, interlacing his fingers atop the old book. "St. Salome's Gospel and Pope Joan's diary could shake the foundations of our faith, altering the Church's history. The voice of women, as Michael indicates these documents suggest, may have been suppressed throughout the centuries. In your perspective, how do you think we should navigate revealing such a profound truth? And what are your thoughts on the repercussions, not just for the Church, but for believers worldwide?"

Hana nodded thoughtfully, appreciating the pope's open-mindedness. "Your Holiness, I think you've hit the nail on the head. As journalists, we deal with truths and their impact every day. It's our job to understand and convey the ripples they cause."

She glanced at the ancient artifacts in the pope's lap. "These documents," she continued, gesturing towards them, "they hold truths that have the potential to drastically reshape our understanding of the Church's past. Their revelation, undoubtedly, will cause turbulence. But it's important to remember that, like all truths, they need to be heard."

She looked earnestly at Pope Ignatius and Michael. "As for the repercussions, they're twofold. For the Church, it means acknowledging and confronting a past that might not align with the established narrative. It might mean turbulence and resistance, yes. But it also offers an opportunity for growth, for reformation. An opportunity to recognize the influence and voices of women who have been largely omitted from Church history.

"For believers worldwide, the impact is personal. It challenges their understanding of their faith. But faith is about truth, and I believe that they can embrace this new truth. It may lead to questions, even doubt, but it could also lead to a deeper understanding and a more inclusive faith. The fear of shaking belief shouldn't prevent the unveiling of truth."

Hana's words, measured and thoughtful, underscored the magnitude of their task. But there was also an undercurrent of optimism, a sense of hopeful anticipation for the changes that these ancient documents could spur in the Church and among its believers.

In opening up the dialogue, Pope Ignatius showed Hana the respect she deserved, acknowledging her valuable insights and her integral role in the journey thus far. Despite the different paths that had led them to this point, they were, in this moment, united by a shared truth, a shared secret that had the power to change history. It was now a collective responsibility, and he recognized the strength that lay in their collaboration.

As the conversation concluded, both Pope Ignatius and Michael Dominic understood the immense challenge that lay before them. Each recognized the need for change, yet also the importance of preserving the Church's history and teachings. It would be a delicate balance, requiring wisdom, patience, and perseverance for the betterment of the Church and the faithful it served.

As they prepared to leave the pope's quarters, Michael and Hana turned back for a final glance at the pope, their eyes meeting the sight of a frail figure lying atop the massive bed in a room shrouded in sacredness and power, his distinctive red slippers a poignant reminder symbolizing the blood of the martyrs who have died for their faith. Died for the very principles and beliefs that their revelations might destroy.

Beneath the lofty ceiling with murals depicting divine scenes, Enrico Petrini, the man who secretly fathered Michael, the man who later become Pope Ignatius, seemed much smaller, almost swallowed by the grandeur of his surroundings. His white cassock, usually so resplendent, appeared to hang loosely on his thinning frame. The strong hands, which had once steadied the Church in times of turbulence, now trembled ever so slightly as they turned the pages of the ancient documents they had brought to him.

His eyes, though, were undimmed—blue orbs that glowed with an intensity that belied his deteriorating health. They reflected a spirit undeterred, a determination unquenched, despite the physical toll time had exacted.

Michael felt a knot tighten in his chest as he watched his mentor lying there. From the time he was a humble parish priest, Petrini had always been a beacon of faith and resilience for him, a spiritual guide whose strength had inspired him. Seeing him now, so vulnerable yet still resolute, filled Michael with a sense of profound respect and a pang of sorrow. Their journey was not just about the historical revelations they were uncovering, but also about the human lives woven into the fabric of this endeavor.

For Hana, the sight of Pope Ignatius was a stark reminder of the human element in her journalism. Here was a man, not just the head of the Catholic Church, but one bearing the weight of history, faith, and now, perhaps, a revolution. As a reporter, she had always tried to separate the person from the position, but in Pope

Ignatius, the two were inseparable. His fragility in the face of impending change was as moving as it was newsworthy. She felt her throat tighten, a lump of emotion for the man who bore his duties with such dignity.

As they closed the door behind them, leaving the Holy Father with his thoughts and the momentous artifacts, they carried with them not just a sense of heavy responsibility, but also the indelible image of a man at the twilight of his life, poised on the brink of what could be a transformative revelation for the Church he so dearly loved.

CHAPTER

EIGHTEEN

As the tranquil evening hues began to dominate the sky, Michael found himself nestled in the serene setting of Santa Maria di Grottaferrata, a monastic relic ensconced in the aroma of pine and moss, nestled among the lush Italian mountains on the outskirts of Rome. This sanctuary seemed a world away from the noise and speed of modern life, a relic preserved in an exquisite capsule of time.

The monks had gone to great lengths to maintain the monastery's secrecy. The exact coordinates were never revealed to Michael. Instead—while carrying Pope Joan's diary and the Salome Gospel he had retrieved from the pope—he was blindfolded and guided into a bulletproof, unmarked vehicle at a pre-arranged pickup spot in Rome. He was then driven on a route that twisted and turned unpredictably through narrow mountain roads and long tunnels, the driver, a silent monk, never once deviating or hesitating. The journey was only part of this ultra secure method of transport.

Once at a specific, seemingly random location, he was transferred to a helicopter, its rotor noise muffled by advanced technology, further ensuring their invisibility. After a disorienting aerial journey, Michael was set down within the hidden walls of the monastery. The blindfold was removed only after they'd securely landed in the seclusion of the monastery's stone courtyard.

Within this hidden retreat, Michael was preparing to execute his strategy, setting his plan into motion for a clandestine meeting with the elusive figure known as Brother Lando Spinosa from the Fellowship of the True Faith.

As a respected scholar specializing in ancient religious texts, Michael had grown accustomed to the hushed reverence of dusty libraries and the excited buzz of groundbreaking discoveries. But his current situation was worlds apart from the conventional academic rigors. He was now entangled in a secret battle with the ominous organization known as the Order of Papal Guardians, directed by the ruthless Lord Pelham, a man bent on manipulating history to his liking.

The monastic tranquility was broken by a low, rumbling grind of ancient stone against stone. An arched door, weathered by centuries, swung open, casting a long, looming shadow across the courtyard. A tall, thin figure emerged, draped in the humble brown habit of his order. His eyes, sharp and sparkling with intelligence, settled on Michael.

"*Buonasera, Padre,*" the man greeted Michael, his voice deep and resonant, as if echoing off the ancient stones surrounding them. His warm smile was comforting, a beacon of light in the hidden darkness, and his handshake was firm yet welcoming. "I am Brother Lando

Spinosa. We appreciate the trust you've placed in us by bringing these invaluable artifacts. Our Fellowship is committed to illuminating the truth, never hiding it."

He paused, his dark eyes filled with sincere regret. "I must also apologize for the circuitous route we took to bring you here," Spinosa continued as he gestured for them to take a seat at a small table in the courtyard. "Our monastery's location is a closely guarded secret, and these measures, while undoubtedly disorienting, are necessary to maintain its sanctity and security. We hope you understand the need for such caution in these uncertain times. Thank you for your understanding and cooperation, Padre."

There was a pause as if Brother Spinosa were waiting for something. Then the cloistered silence was gently interrupted by the soft patter of sandaled feet against the cobblestones. A younger monk, Brother Matteo, emerged from the arched entranceway leading to the monastery's inner chambers. Framed by the ancient stone doorway, he seemed almost like a figure from a Renaissance painting, a splash of warm humanity set against the cool austerity of the monastery's architecture.

Cloaked in the same humble habit as Spinosa but with a woolen shawl draped over his shoulders to ward off the light chill of the evening, Matteo cradled a wooden tray with the utmost reverence. On it sat a traditional Italian Moka pot, its sides gleaming softly in the fading light. Nestled beside it were two earthenware cups, their simple design a testament to the monastery's minimalist aesthetic. A faint, comforting aroma trailed behind him, the unmistakable scent of freshly brewed tea mingling with the ancient scent of the stones.

His youthful face was serene, touched with the soft

amber glow of the setting sun. With every step, his eyes, sparkling with unspoken wisdom beyond his years, remained respectfully downcast. As he neared Michael and Brother Spinosa, he raised his gaze, offering them a small, genuine smile—the universal language of shared camaraderie.

"Brothers," he greeted them, his voice a melodious whisper carried on the mountain breeze. He extended the tray toward them. The smell of the tea, a blend of local herbs and wild honey collected from the nearby woods, was soothing, an olfactory balm to the tensions of the day.

With a practiced hand, Matteo balanced the tray with one hand and poured the tea with the other, the liquid a golden-amber hue, the steam dancing up in the cool air. The delicate clink of the cups as he served them was the only sound that punctuated the hushed reverence of the moment. This simple act of hospitality was a testament to the timeless rituals of the monastery, serving as a grounding force amidst the brewing storm of intrigue and danger.

Once Brother Matteo departed, the lingering silence was broken as Brother Spinosa began to recount his knowledge of Lord Pelham. "My dear Michael," he began, the echo of the stone walls resonating with the somber tone of his voice. "Our Fellowship may seem out of place in this world of secrecy and power plays, yet we have survived centuries through our vigilance. We live in seclusion, not ignorance."

Spinosa's gaze shifted to the distant hills, the fading light of the sun casting an ethereal glow on his face. "Lord Pelham," he continued, "is a man of vast influence and unyielding ambition. As the head of the OPG, he commands a network of individuals who share his goal of controlling historical narratives for their gain."

Spinosa's familiarity with such a man seemed to contrast with his monastic life. Noticing Michael's quizzical expression, he added, "We've long known about the OPG. An old adversary of the Fellowship, one could say. Over the centuries, our paths have crossed, always in defense of truth. We've kept a close eye on their activities, and when Lord Pelham rose to leadership, his ruthless pursuit of power set off alarm bells."

"The Fellowship," Spinosa continued, "relies on a network of informants, many of whom live ordinary lives yet remain true to our cause. They keep us abreast of the OPG's movements. It was through one such informant that we first learned of your discovery.

"Your decision to protect these treasures," Spinosa continued, admiration echoing in his voice, "has brought you into a world few ever glimpse. But know this, Michael, the Fellowship stands with you. We've walked this path before."

Indeed, for a group of seemingly austere monks, Michael soon came to realize that the Fellowship of the True Faith bore the dual nature of both the silent sentinel and the cunning fox. Hidden within the sanctity of their monastic life was a subtle undercurrent of vigilance and technological prowess, enabling them to guard history's truths against those who sought to manipulate them.

Before Spinosa lay the artifacts Michael had shared with the Holy Father just the day before: Pope Joan's diary, a humble leather-bound tome, its pages filled with ornate Anglo-Saxon script that held the potential to redefine history, and the illuminating Gospel of St. Salome, a

unique relic that narrated the overlooked apostle's experiences.

Spinosa looked at the artifacts with quiet awe, an air
of sanctity surrounding him. He reached to the side and
took a blank piece of parchment from a nearby stack,
setting it carefully beside the Gospel of Salome. He then
retrieved an exquisitely carved wooden box, its interior
lined with plush velvet. Nestled within was a pair of
gloves, a seamless and lightweight fabric that shimmered
with a metallic sheen, clearly made of some advanced,
near alien material. "These are our Order's crowning
treasure," Spinosa explained, "These gloves can transfer
text from one surface to another, without requiring physical contact. This allows us to create a perfect facsimile of
any document we choose."

Noting Michael's surprise, Spinosa added, "Yes, I too
would be startled if I were in your position. As it
happens, one of our benefactors is a high-technology
magnate in Silicon Valley. It is to him we owe a great
debt for enabling our mission with such wondrous
science, not to mention what resources we might need to
fulfill our mission."

Donning the gloves, Spinosa ran his hands gently
above the ancient text, and a miracle unfolded. The blank
parchment beside the Gospel began to fill with lines of
text, mirroring exactly what was written in the original
artifacts. He repeated the actions with the remaining
pages of the artifacts while explaining, "These copies will
be used to draw the attention of the OPG, while the real
treasures will be kept secure wherever you wish to keep
them."

Next, Spinosa produced an intricate device, not much
larger than a pocket watch, but pulsating with hidden

complexity. Its needle, haphazardly spinning, found direction as it neared the artifacts, pointing to a microscopically small symbol etched onto them. "These are tracking sigils," Spinosa explained. "We can turn Lord Pelham's tricks against him."

Michael cocked his head, intrigued. A sigil was traditionally a pictorial symbol used in ritualistic magic and supposed to have supernatural power, yet clearly technological magic of sorts was at play here. Spinosa then revealed a seemingly unremarkable fragment of an ancient stone tablet. However, as he brought the device near it, the needle adjusted, pointing unwaveringly toward the tablet. "These sigils can be programmed to misdirect. While Lord Pelham's agents pursue false leads, you may transport or retain the genuine artifacts safely."

Michael marveled at the sophistication and precision of Brother Spinosa's plan—a blend of ancient traditions, advanced technology, and strategic cunning. It was an oasis of hope amidst his fears. He knew then that with the Fellowship of the True Faith as his allies, Lord Pelham and his Order wouldn't be able to suppress the past so easily.

Or so he hoped.

CHAPTER
NINETEEN

O n a drizzly London morning, the anticipation in the air was nearly palpable. It was not an ordinary day. The British Museum was about to make an announcement, one that promised to shape the course of historical discourse. The expansive foyer of the museum was abuzz with life, an excited chatter filling the air as journalists, historians, and dignitaries from around the globe huddled, waiting for the revelation. The event was broadcast live, streaming to millions of screens around the world, amplifying the anticipation tenfold.

At the heart of this electric atmosphere was a grand podium, veiled in rich, sapphire velvet. Amid this congregation of eager faces, Lady Imogen Harper, the esteemed chair of the Board of Trustees of the British Museum, made her entrance. A formidable presence, she was a woman of exceptional intellect and charismatic disposition, a combination that had made her a revered figure in the field of history.

"Ladies and gentlemen," she commenced, her resonant voice filling the high-ceilinged hall. "We stand on
the brink of a remarkable revelation, one that promises to
redefine our understanding of history and faith."

Pausing for dramatic effect, she allowed the growing
suspense to permeate the room. "The *Echoes of Faith* exhibition," she continued, "has always aimed to celebrate
our shared historical legacy, revealing the intricacies and
nuances of our shared past. This year, we endeavor to
push the boundaries of historical exploration even
further.

"Today, it is with great honor that we announce the
late addition of two remarkable, enigmatic artifacts that
have recently come to light. Artifacts that promise to
unveil a riveting chapter of historical narrative that has
been, until now, shrouded in the shadows of time."

A collective gasp swept across the room as Lady
Imogen let her words hang in the air, leaving her audi-
ence to absorb the magnitude of her statement. The
grand room was filled with a mix of excited murmurs
and speculative whispers, the buzzing undercurrent
amplifying the atmosphere of suspense.

Simultaneously, the grand screen behind her flickered
to life. It showcased a silhouette of two items—their
identities obscured, adding to the mystery. "These artifacts promise to unveil an unprecedented shift in our
understanding of ancient narratives. However, the
specifics will remain shrouded in mystery until the day
of the exhibition."

Finally, Lady Imogen concluded, the warmth in her
voice replaced by an undeniable edge of excitement,
"Join us on the twenty-fifth of this month to bear witness
to a revelation like no other. The *Echoes of Faith* exhibition

isn't merely a faint whisper from history, but a thunderous clamor resonating through the annals of time that brings to light a new path into our future!"

As she stepped down from the stage, the room erupted into applause and chatter. The anticipation swept out from the grand museum hall, propagating through the city streets, the country, and out into the wider world. The upcoming *Echoes of Faith* exhibition was now not just a date in the diary but a global event, a moment of unveiling that held the world in breathless anticipation.

∽

IN THE QUIET solitude of his oceanfront estate, far removed from the bustling energy of London, Lord Pelham sat ensconced in his grand study. The room, with its rich mahogany paneling and towering bookcases filled with volumes of history and lore, reflected its owner's obsession with the past. Against this backdrop, the flickering light of the tall fireplace cast a play of light and shadow, lending an air of dramatic intensity to the room.

The only other illumination in the room came from a large, high-definition television screen that dominated one wall. The live broadcast from the British Museum filled the room, Lady Imogen Harper's confident proclamation echoing in the high-ceilinged study. As he listened to her carefully crafted announcement, his sharp, hawk-like eyes narrowed in thought, his jaw tightening.

The rhythmical drumming of his fingers against the

worn leather of his armchair was the only sound that dared compete with Harper's voice. His gaze was steely, intense. He knew what these 'surprise artifacts' were. They were *his* artifacts. Or, at least, they were meant to be.

A cold, cruel smile curled his lips, the spark in his eyes hardening into something akin to flint. He reached for the phone set on his desk, his fingers deftly dialing a number he knew by heart. As the recipient on the other end picked up, his voice was a silky purr. "It seems our esteemed friends at the British Museum are planning a little surprise," he began, the threat behind his words as tangible as the antique bronze statue that graced his desk.

"Yes," came the curt response from his head of operations, a man known only as Trask. There was no surprise in his tone; he too had seen the announcement.

"Good," Pelham replied, his voice a dangerous whisper. "I want those artifacts, Trask. I don't care what it takes. They are key to stopping whatever plans they may have. We must secure them."

"Understood. I'll assemble a team." Trask's voice was crisp, professional. They had been in similar situations before.

As Pelham hung up the phone, his mind whirred into action. The prospect of the artifacts being in such a public place as the British Museum had never crossed his mind. But it was not entirely unwelcome. Despite the museum's extensive security systems, they also had predictable patterns, patterns that could be exploited.

A meticulous plan began to form in his mind, a cat and mouse game of precision and stealth. He would need to act fast, yet discreetly, to ensure his organization's cover remained intact. Confidence surged through him as he reclined in his chair, the cruel smile never leaving his face. The *Echoes of Faith* exhibition was about to take on a whole new meaning. In the grand tapestry of history, he was about to leave his indelible mark.

TWENTY

T he rustic charm of the Swiss Guard barracks was a stark contrast to the ornate splendor of the rest of Vatican City. The locker room, filled with the usual clatter and banter of guards changing shifts, was suddenly silenced by the entrance of Karl Dengler and Lukas Bischoff. Both had just returned from holiday and were met with jovial greetings, but their expressions were uncharacteristically somber.

Felix Bauer, a fellow Swiss Guard known for his brash demeanor and imposing figure, was sitting on the bench, lacing up his boots. As Karl and Lukas approached him, a tense silence fell over the room. The other guards, sensing the shift in atmosphere, discreetly retreated, leaving the trio alone.

Lukas, his blue eyes hard with determination, broke the silence. "Felix, were you driving a red VW sedan following us the other night?" he asked, his voice steady.

Bauer stiffened, his normally confident demeanor wavering under the direct question. He threw Lukas a dangerous glare, his clenched jaw betraying his growing irritation. "Why would you ask that, Lukas?" he retorted, trying to mask his guilt with a layer of indignant defiance.

There was a ripple of tension. Karl and Lukas exchanged a look. Karl's heart pounded in his chest, the memory of the red VW and the bullets whizzing past his head still fresh in his mind. He remembered the fear in Michael's and Hana's eyes as he drove them away from the airport. The realization that Bauer might be responsible for that night's terror sent a wave of betrayal through him, the collegial treasure of a longtime friendship vanishing in a moment's action.

Lukas, feeling the same sense of disillusionment, stood his ground. He had always known Bauer to be aggressive, even volatile, but to think he could be involved in an attempt on their lives was unthinkable.

"Your defensiveness is answer enough, Bauer," Karl said, his voice ringing out with undisguised bitterness. His eyes met Bauer's, the silent accusation hanging heavy in the air.

Bauer, now realizing he was cornered, visibly bristled. His usual braggadocio replaced by a dangerous, feral-like edge. He rose to his feet, his imposing frame casting an ominous shadow. "You accusing me of something?" he challenged, his hand balling into a fist. His brown eyes flared with anger, yet beneath it, fear flickered.

Lukas and Karl stood unwavering, their shared sense of betrayal fueling their courage. They knew they were accusing one of their own, but the loyalty they felt for their fellow guards didn't extend to traitors. They were prepared for the fallout, their resolve unbroken, their expressions resolute.

Bauer's eyes darted between the two men, a small bead of sweat trickling down the side of his face. Silence stretched between them, the stillness disrupted only by the occasional scrape of a boot against the concrete floor.

The standoff continued, the silence stretching uncomfortably long. But, none of them was ready to back down from an emotional gridlock with no clear resolution in sight.

Then, suddenly, the loud echo of a gong sounded throughout the barracks, signaling the changing of the guard. The mundane, familiar noise felt strangely jarring amidst the tense atmosphere. It served as a reminder of their duty and responsibility—a call they couldn't ignore, no matter the personal turmoil brewing inside the locker room.

Karl and Lukas, their gaze never leaving Bauer, slowly backed away. "This isn't over, Bauer," Karl said, his voice a low growl. The warning hung in the air, clear as a bell.

Bauer, feeling a momentary reprieve, shot back, "Be careful with your accusations, Karl. You're playing with fire." His words were laden with a thinly veiled threat, adding another layer to the already complex, tension-filled atmosphere.

With one final look of shared understanding, Karl and Lukas turned and left, leaving Bauer standing alone amidst the abandoned locker room. The door swung shut behind them, enclosing Bauer in a silence that was more condemning than any words could be.

The confrontation had ended, but it was clear that the real battle was just beginning. Trust was shattered, lines were drawn, and the usually cohesive Swiss Guard was on the brink of internal conflict. The lingering question— the mystery of the red VW sedan—remained unresolved, a dangerous seed of doubt planted in the heart of the barracks. There was no resolution, only the promise of a storm brewing on the horizon.

CHAPTER

TWENTY-ONE

I t was a dark, rain-slicked morning in Dorset, the kind of gray morning that feels like twilight. The pattering of rain on the precinct roof was a monotonous drumbeat that Detective Inspector Grace Dempsey could feel down to her bones, a rhythm of tension and impending discovery. She held in her hands a small, plastic evidence bag containing a beautifully crafted medallion, the symbol of the Order of Papal Guardians embossed on one side and an Ouroboros on the other.

Dempsey was a seasoned investigator, her eyes mirroring the battles she had fought with crime over the years, etched with the weight of the lives she had worked tirelessly to get justice for. She was often told that her best tool was her relentless determination, and in this particular case, it was this grit that had led to the crucial discovery of a single fingerprint on the medallion's polished surface.

As she peered at the precious piece of evidence

through the magnifying lens of her desk lamp, her mind raced with the possible implications. The medallion must be significant, its symbolism yet to be understood. Its presence on Reverend Andrews' body was a cryptic anomaly that had nagged at her since the discovery. Now, with the added detail of the fingerprint, a new lead had emerged in the case.

She had enlisted the help of the Forensic team to run the print through Interpol's AFIS international finger-print database, and as the night drew on, she found herself staring at her phone, willing it to ring. When it did, the sharp trill cut through the silence of the early hours like a knife.

"Hold on," she said, scribbling down the results from the other end of the line. She felt a strange sensation in the pit of her stomach as she wrote the name down, disbelief and a kind of gnawing dread. She thanked the forensic analyst, ended the call, and stared blankly at the name scrawled on the notepad in front of her.

Karl Dengler. Sergeant. Vatican Swiss Guard.

Dempsey felt a chill run down her spine. Dengler was known to her, not as a suspect but as one of Father Michael Dominic's closest associates. An unlikely figure to be implicated in such a grisly murder. Father Dominic had clearly stated that although Sergeant Dengler had examined the body and discovered the coin, that the sergeant had handled the coin strictly with his jacket cuff, by the edges. If true, there would be no fingerprint. So either Dengler had killed Andrews prior to Father Dominic discovering the body and witnessing the sergeant's moves, or the good Father himself had lied.

She leaned back in her chair, cradling the medallion

in her hand once again. The story it had to tell was one she wasn't expecting.

It was time for her team to explore this new angle, this unforeseen complication. They would have to dig deeper into Dengler's connection with Reverend Andrews, into his relationship with Father Michael, and perhaps even into the inner workings of the Order itself, if that was even possible.

Dempsey knew then, it was going to be a long day. Little did she know, however, that strings were being pulled from afar by hands of deceit and a mind of manipulation—that of the cunning Lord Pelham. But that was a revelation yet to dawn. For now, her focus was on the unexpected suspect, the trusted Swiss Guard who discovered the body, Karl Dengler.

THE MORNING WAS misty and overcast when Michael Dominic and Hana Sinclair arrived at Rome's Fiumicino Airport. The mood in the air was a mirror of their own—a murky mix of anticipation, anxiety, and determination. It wasn't the first time they were flying back to London, but it felt different this time around.

In their possession were two faux artifacts—the diary of Pope Joan and the Gospel of St. Salome—crafted with meticulous precision by Brother Spinosa's wondrous high-tech glove. A feat of remarkable duplicity meant to outwit a man notorious for his cunning—Lord Lucius Pelham.

In the hushed whisper of the jet engines, Michael turned to Hana. "Once we deliver these to the British Museum, it'll be only a matter of time before Pelham and his minions make a move," he said, his gaze locked on the horizon outside.

Hana nodded, her fingers nervously flipping through her reporter's notebook. "I've alerted my contact in Scotland Yard. They're preparing to monitor the museum discreetly to see when and how Pelham sets his plan in motion."

Their conversation drifted to the events that had led them to this point—discovering the actual artifacts in Sherborne Abbey, the terrifying encounter with Lord Pelham, the death of Reverend Andrews, the harrowing experience of their brakes failing in the rental car, and the virulent car chase through the frenetic streets of Rome.

As the cityscape of London came into view, they steeled themselves for the task at hand. Once landed, they headed straight to the British Museum. The grandeur of the building was a stark contrast to the deceptive mission they were on.

THE BRITISH MUSEUM buzzed with the quiet hum of visitors murmuring and echoing footfalls, the air filled with a palpable sense of reverence. Father Michael Dominic walked through the imposing entrance, a guarded case under his arm—the decoy artifacts Brother Lando Spinosa had created to fool Lord Pelham's prying eyes.

Beside him, Hana Sinclair walked with a journalist's sharp eye, scanning the surroundings and subtly checking for anyone who might be paying undue attention to their arrival.

They made their way to the Egyptian Gallery, where Michael was to deliver the decoy artifacts. In the marble halls of the museum, they were met by Skyler Armitage, the head curator. With a display of normalcy that belied their tension, they handed over the replicated artifacts. Skyler, in awe of what he believed to be the original pieces, promised to accord them the highest security. The irony of his statement wasn't lost on Michael and Hana.

After leaving the case with the curator, Michael suggested they take a moment to peruse the museum. Hana agreed, intrigued by the notion of exploring the grand institution's treasures alongside Michael.

They found themselves standing before a large painting of the Madonna, her eyes filled with divine sorrow and boundless love. Michael looked at it with a priest's reverence, seeing in it the embodiment of his life-long commitment to his faith.

"Hana," he said, his voice soft, "look at her eyes, the duality of her emotions. There's sorrow and joy, loss and fulfillment. A lot like our journey, don't you think?"

Hana looked at the painting, then at Michael, noticing the similar duality in his eyes. He was right. Their journey was filled with that same mix of emotions—loss and discovery, dread and hope.

"It is," Hana admitted. "But it's not just the duality, Michael. It's about resilience too. We face our trials, but we persist. Just like she did," she said, gesturing towards the painting.

Michael looked at Hana, her eyes filled with determi-nation, mirroring the resilience she spoke of. A pang of admiration stirred within him. Their relationship might be complicated by his vows and her journalistic impar-tiality, but their shared respect and the unspoken bond between them were undeniably strong.

They continued to walk through the museum, stopping at various paintings and sculptures, each inspiring profound conversations about faith, commitment, and the human spirit. They spoke of martyrs and saints, ancient civilizations, and the universal threads of humanity woven into the tapestry of time.

As Michael and Hana lingered before the famed Rosetta Stone exhibit, they discussed the power of language. The stone, the key to deciphering Egyptian hieroglyphics, and thus a bridge to an ancient civilization, fascinated them both.

"Language," Michael mused, "is the tool by which we share our beliefs, hopes, and fears. It can unite us or divide us. Like our faith, it needs to be understood, not just spoken." Hana listened, her journalistic mind drawn to the essence of Michael's words—the power of understanding. It was a reflection of their own journey, their efforts to understand the clues and narratives that led them here.

Next, they found themselves amid a collection of religious texts. There were scriptures from various faiths, each representing a different perspective of divinity. "It's interesting," Hana said, "how faith can have so many faces, yet at its core, it seeks to answer the same existential questions." Michael nodded, appreciating the depth of her insight, seeing in her words a reflection of their own faith—the faith in their mission, the faith in each other.

They then stopped before a statue of Sappho, the famed ancient poetess. Her stone figure stood as a testament to the voice of women, echoing through history, resilient and influential. "The Church could learn from history," Michael suggested, hinting at their shared hope for the Church's future recognition of women. "Women like Sappho had a profound impact despite societal constraints. Imagine the potential if those barriers were removed." Hana agreed, her thoughts already drifting towards her next article.

As they were about to leave, they found themselves before a sculpture that took their breath away—two figures captured in an eternal dance, their forms intertwined, their faces tantalizingly close, yet not touching. It was a beautiful representation of a dance of desire or a lament of separation.

They fell silent, the sculpture eerily mirroring their relationship—a dance between the sacred vows of a priest and the unbiased commitments of a journalist. A dance that had brought them so close yet held them apart. The sculpture's silent narration of unfulfilled desires and unexpressed feelings resonated with their own unspoken emotions.

"Sometimes," Michael broke the silence, his voice barely above a whisper, "art echoes life in ways we can't express ourselves." He didn't look at Hana, but his words hung heavy in the air between them.

Hana glanced at Michael, his profile strong against the dim museum lighting. "And sometimes," she said, a soft, wistful smile playing on her lips, "it speaks the words we can't say out loud." She too was looking at the sculpture, her voice a mere whisper in the grand museum hall.

With a final, lingering look at the intertwined figures, they walked out of the museum, the echoes of their silent conversation resonating in the vacated space, a testament to their unfulfilled desire, unstated feelings, and unspoken bond.

TWENTY-TWO

As dusk fell over London, Trask stood in the shadows, cloaked by the encroaching darkness. He overlooked the grand edifice of the British Museum, his sharp gaze dissecting its every detail. He'd spent the past week studying the museum's blueprints, security protocols, and patterns of human behavior. It was time to set his meticulously crafted plan into action.

Trask and his team had painstakingly sculpted latex masks of their faces and used advanced prosthetics to change their body structures. They had blended in with the crowd as common museum visitors. Their clothes hid an assortment of devices—miniature jammers, fiber-optic cameras, and laser cutters—each piece of equipment carefully selected to overcome specific security obstacles.

Earlier in the day, a separate team had secretly released nano-drones into the museum's ventilation system. These tiny machines were equipped with multi-spectrum cameras and were virtually undetectable. They'd provided a real-time feed of the entire museum's layout, security positions, and, most importantly, the locations of the two artifacts. This data was now being streamed to Trask and his team's AR, or Augmented Reality, glasses, enabling them to navigate the museum while avoiding security personnel and cameras.

As the museum announced its closing time, Trask's team strategically lagged behind, using their AR glasses to monitor positions of museum security personnel and thus avoid discovery while they found places to hide. Meanwhile, a member of Trask's team who was an expert in electronics surreptitiously attached a tiny microjammer to the museum's main control room exterior. This device was designed to disrupt the communication between the alarm system and the security guards for precisely one hundred twenty seconds—enough time to steal the artifacts and disappear without triggering any alarms.

Trask signaled his team, and they all slipped on gloves coated with a specialized film that replicated human skin but left no fingerprints. It was time to move.

Using a portable scanner hidden in his sleeve, Trask scanned the locking mechanism on the exhibit case. It was a biometric system tied to a handful of museum curators. The device intercepted the biometric data of one of the curators from earlier in the day, replicating it to bypass the lock.

With a soft click, the exhibit case unlocked. Inside were the artifacts—the diary of Pope Joan and the Gospel of St. Salome. The sight of them made Trask pause. They were pieces of history, powerful symbols of a past that had been carefully hidden. But to him, and to Lord Pelham, they were merely tools for a larger purpose.

Trask reached out, his hand steady. However, he

didn't touch the artifacts directly. Instead, he used a pair of extraction rods—non-abrasive and electrostatically neutral to prevent any damage or contamination. As soon as the artifacts were clear of the pressure-sensitive platform, another team member quickly replaced them with precise replicas based on unique specifications gleaned from Pelham's contacts in the museum. These replicas were made from a unique polymer blend and filled with a ferrofluid that perfectly matched the weight and electromagnetic signature of the original artifacts, effectively tricking the security system.

With the artifacts safely enclosed in specially designed cases, Trask and his team began their exit. They moved through the museum like ghosts, their every action synchronized to the second. As they exited the main hall, the microjammer was deactivated and retrieved, and communication was restored to the control room. The museum's security system remained none the wiser.

Outside, a nondescript van waited, blending seamlessly with the evening cityscape. The driver, an expert in evasive and defensive driving, navigated the labyrinth of London streets effortlessly. The team knew the city's CCTV network inside and out, and the van was equipped with an array of devices to disrupt the tracking systems, should the need arise.

As the van disappeared into the city's bustle, the British Museum stood as grand and undisturbed as ever, oblivious to the heist that had just occurred under its illustrious roof. It would be hours before anyone realized that the priceless artifacts, the crown jewels of the *Echoes of Faith* exhibition, were nothing more than expertly crafted replicas. By then, Trask and his team, along with the artifacts, would be long gone. The perfect heist had been executed without a hitch.

THE METROPOLITAN POLICE surveillance team was hidden in an unmarked van parked casually on Great Russell Street. The van provided a panoramic view of the British Museum's main entrance, an ideally inconspicuous position for a covert operation. The van's interior was a hub of activity, an array of screens lighting up the faces of the assembled officers. They watched the live feed from the hidden cameras inside the museum, their attention riveted on the unfolding drama.

Detective Chief Inspector Graham Harris was leading the operation. He was a tall, weathered man with a reputation for being methodical and relentless. He adjusted his headset and leaned closer to the screen showing Trask and his men inside the museum.

"Alright, they're on the move," he announced, the tension in his voice conspicuous.

Everyone in the van was on high alert as they watched Trask and his team executing their meticulously planned theft. The officers tracked every step, from the diversion in the Egyptian exhibit to the swift acquisition of the fake artifacts.

As Trask and his team exited the museum, an officer from the back of the van updated Harris. "The GPS tracker has been activated, sir. We've got a lock on their vehicle."

"Good," Harris said, his eyes never leaving the screen. "Keep monitoring them. Let them believe they've gotten away with it."

As the surveillance van discreetly followed Trask's

vehicle, DCI Harris contacted his team stationed at various points throughout the city. "All units, stay on standby. Let them move, let them breathe, but don't lose them."

The adrenaline was palpable in the van. Every officer knew the importance of their operation and the stakes involved. They also knew the brilliance of the man they were dealing with. Lord Pelham was cunning and ruthless, and his operative, Trask, was no less dangerous.

They watched as Trask's vehicle blended into London's night traffic, making its way out of the city centre. Harris kept an eye on the GPS tracker, its blinking light following Trask's vehicle as it moved farther away from the museum.

"Let them go," he said finally, pulling off his headset and turning to his team. "The real game has just begun."

The surveillance operation continued, Scotland Yard now playing a dangerous game of cat and mouse with some of England's most formidable adversaries. The police had allowed the theft, their greater goal in sight— unmasking the larger conspiracy, arresting Lord Pelham, and protecting the secrets that could change the face of the Church forever.

CHAPTER
TWENTY-THREE

Lord Pelham's stately oceanfront mansion in Lyme Regis stood isolated, its architectural grandeur standing in stark contrast to the wild, untamed beauty of the Jurassic Coast. As night fell, the mansion's gleaming windows mirrored the play of the moonlight on the churning waves below, casting an eerie, silvery glow over the scene.

Trask drove up the winding cliffside road, maneuvering the sleek, black Jaguar XF with the precision of a man who knew the route by heart. As he brought the car to a smooth halt in front of the mansion's entrance, the large oak doors swung open, revealing Pelham's tall figure looming in the doorway. The silhouetted figure emanated an air of power and an almost tangible sense of anticipation.

"I trust your mission was successful?" Pelham's voice resonated through the crisp sea air, the smile in his voice undeniable.

"Indeed, my lord," Trask responded, stepping out of

the car. He carried a secured, unassuming case—the ordinary exterior hiding the priceless treasures within.

Pelham led Trask through the opulent mansion, down an ornately decorated corridor to a study that overlooked the sea. The room, bathed in the soft glow of a fireplace, was filled with artifacts and relics from different eras and cultures—a testament to Pelham's longstanding obsession with history.

Pelham took a seat behind a grand desk, crafted from dark mahogany and adorned with ornate carvings. The soft flicker of the fire played upon his face, his eyes twinkling with an almost childlike delight. "Show me," he demanded, his voice barely more than a whisper, betraying his growing excitement.

With a nod, Trask placed the case on the desk and unlocked it. As he opened the case, the diary of Pope Joan and the Gospel of St. Salome were revealed. Their worn, ancient surfaces seemed to shimmer in the firelight, an aura of immense historical significance surrounding them.

Pelham reached out, his gloved hands trembling slightly as he touched the artifacts. His breath hitched in his throat as he gently picked up the diary, its worn leather and brittle pages belying the secrets it held. "Extraordinary," he murmured, his gaze traveling over the delicate, ancient script.

Next, he turned his attention to the Gospel of St. Salome. As he traced his fingers over the time-worn parchment, a sense of triumph washed over him. The acquisition of these artifacts marked a significant victory, not just against the Fellowship of the True Faith, but also in his quest for power.

"Congratulations are in order, Trask," he said, his

eyes never leaving the Gospel. "Your execution was flaw-less. Your team has outdone themselves." There was genuine admiration in his voice, but it was swiftly over-shadowed by his obsession with the relics before him.

Pelham spent hours inspecting the artifacts, getting lost in the ancient texts. The diary and the gospel were not just artifacts to him; they were keys to unlocking untapped power, power that he intended to harness. As he pored over them, he felt a surge of exhilaration.

Outside, the waves crashed against the cliffs, a symphony of raw, natural power underlining the silent, insidious plot unfolding within the mansion's walls. The world remained oblivious to the shift in power, the balance of history teetering on the brink of a precipice. But for Lord Pelham, it was a moment of sweet victory, a moment where he reveled in his success and the tanta-lizing promise of a future he was on the brink of commanding. His gaze on the artifacts, he murmured into the quiet room, "The game has only just begun."

DEEP within the heart of Rome, hidden amidst the tranquility of the Santa Maria di Grottaferrata monastery, the members of the Fellowship of the True Faith gathered around a low table. The gentle flicker of candlelight cast dancing shadows over the ancient stone walls, the room filled with an air of expectant silence.

Michael Dominic, Brother Lando Spinosa, and several other monks huddled close, their eyes fixed on a small holographic display projected from a device in the center of the table. It showed a glowing dot steadily moving towards the western coast of England, a direct signal from the tracking sigils embedded within the replicas.

As the dot came to a halt at Lyme Regis, a collective gasp echoed around the table. A wide grin spread across Michael's face as he turned towards Brother Spinosa. "He's taken the bait," he exclaimed, his voice a mixture of relief and triumph.

The room burst into a flurry of excited whispers and back-slapping, the monks' usually composed demeanor momentarily forgotten. The carefully executed plan had worked—their invaluable artifacts remained safe, and the treacherous Lord Pelham had walked right into their trap.

With the air of celebration momentarily subsiding, Brother Spinosa raised his hand, commanding silence. The room instantly fell quiet, every eye turning to the old monk. "This is only the beginning," he reminded them, his voice carrying the wisdom of his years. "We must alert the authorities without alerting Pelham."

Michael nodded in agreement, his jubilant expression sobering. Reaching into his pocket, he produced a cell phone. A deep breath steadied him as he dialed a number, a direct line to Sir Harold Attenborough, the Executive Director of the British Museum. It had been a carefully cultivated relationship, built on trust and mutual respect, and tonight it would be put to the test.

As the line connected, Michael launched into a brief, coded conversation, skirting around explicit details while conveying the necessary information on the assumption Pelham's arsenal included call interceptions. "It appears your *Echoes of Faith* have found their way to the Jurassic Coast," he hinted.

Understanding dawned on Attenborough with a mix

of shock and anger. *Pelham*, he silently seethed, his suspicions confirmed.

Michael didn't need to reply. The silence was confirmation enough. A flurry of promises followed. The British authorities would be alerted immediately. They would bring Pelham to justice, recover the artifacts, and ensure the true culprits were caught.

After the call ended, Michael returned his attention to the group, the gravity of the situation settling in. "They'll handle it from here," he reassured them, his gaze meeting each pair of eyes in the room.

The room once again erupted in muted celebration. There was still danger, still a chance that Pelham could slip through their fingers, but for now, they had won a significant battle. Their clever ruse had paid off, and the priceless artifacts remained safely hidden in the depths of the monastery.

Lord Pelham, with his vast resources and unyielding determination, was not a man easily outwitted. But for tonight, they had won, and that was a victory they would savor.

CHAPTER
TWENTY-FOUR

While the Fellowship of the True Faith celebrated their perceived victory in the hills of Rome, a storm was brewing on the windswept coast of West Dorset. Within the opulent walls of his seaside mansion, Lord Pelham pondered his situation.

Pelham, seated in his study with the replicas of the artifacts in front of him, contemplated his next move. Something about the situation had begun to unsettle him. His eyes, sharp and piercing, scrutinized the replicas, studying them with a growing sense of unease. As he pondered, his fingers traced the pages of the Gospel, and he found the texture... off.

A sudden realization sparked in his mind. His gaze narrowed as he reached for a handheld scanner from his desk drawer. A few passes over the replicas confirmed his suspicion. They were perfect in weight and appearance but lacked the expected electromagnetic signatures of ancient parchment and leather.

A slow, cold smile spread across Pelham's face as he understood the depth of the deceit. His laugh, bitter and cynical, echoed in the silence of the study. He had been played. But rather than anger, he felt a surge of thrill. The game had become interesting.

Immediately, he summoned Trask. As his trusted associate entered the room, Pelham tossed him the Gospel replica. "What does this tell you?" he asked, his gaze fixed on the subordinate.

Trask examined the artifact, his face quickly mirroring the realization Pelham had moments earlier. "By your reaction I assume these are fakes?" he stated, looking up at Pelham with a grave expression.

Instead of responding, Pelham turned to a hidden wall panel, his fingers swiftly punching in a code. The panel slid back to reveal an array of advanced technological devices. Among them was a small, sleek machine—a high-tech artifact scanner capable of detecting even the faintest residual energy patterns. He picked it up and ran it over the replicas.

The machine beeped softly, the screen lighting up with faint traces of the sigils embedded in the fakes. Pelham's smile widened. The Fellowship, the only organization clever enough to be behind this ruse, had made one critical mistake—they underestimated him.

"Your Lordship," Trask began, unsure of his master's sudden amusement amidst their predicament, "what's the plan?"

Pelham turned to Trask, the fire in his eyes reflecting a newfound determination. "We play their game, Trask. Only this time, we change the rules."

Lord Pelham immediately initiated a comprehensive counter-operation. He contacted his tech expert, instructing him to reverse-engineer the tracking sigils, a task that would ordinarily take weeks, but time was a luxury they didn't have, and he quickly committed to the exorbitant funds required to expedite the process.

Meanwhile, he sent out his intelligence network to find any possible leads on the Fellowship's location. Every resource he had was employed—from satellite surveillance to deep web informants. He wasn't just planning to retrieve the artifacts; he was waging war on the Fellowship.

Simultaneously, he alerted his legal team, instructing them to prepare for any potential allegations from the British authorities. He knew it was a matter of time before they'd come knocking, but he intended to be ready.

As the night grew darker, the mansion turned into a hub of frantic activity. Lord Pelham stood at the helm, orchestrating every move with calculated precision. He knew the challenge was monumental, the risks high. But his resolve was unyielding.

Pelham was no ordinary adversary. He was a seasoned player in this deadly game of power and deceit. He understood the stakes, the moves, and the players. He knew the night was just the beginning of a tumultuous battle. But he was ready.

Because when it came to the game of power, Lord Pelham never lost. And he wasn't about to start now.

PELHAM SCRUTINIZED the meticulously planned defensive measures sprawled across the table; defensive measures he could employ only after locating the monastery. He knew the monastery was a fortress hidden away from prying eyes by a vast expanse of wilderness and sheer geographic isolation. But where?

Beside him, Trask stood in silence, knowing better than to disturb his master's concentration.

The sanctuary, home to the Fellowship of the True Faith, had been a mystery to the OPG for centuries. Its location was carefully kept secret, concealed by an impenetrable network of loyal and silent brethren who had taken vows to protect the sanctity of their home. Pelham had long since realized that they took advantage of a rugged terrain and the remote location to make it invisible to ordinary satellite surveillance, otherwise he would have located it long ago.

Pelham had, in the past, employed every resource at his disposal to uncover the monastery's location, but to no avail. Despite their tireless efforts, the exact location of the monastery remained elusive.

Now, aided by the embedded sigils, Pelham's tech expert labored to decipher the coordinates encrypted in the fake documents. As the hours ticked by, Pelham's phone buzzed with an incoming message. His lips twitched into a smile as he read the message: they had cracked the encrypted documents. The location, however, pointed to a remote mountainous region with many possible hiding places. This was not going to be a simple mission.

He turned to Trask, determination flaring in his eyes. "Prepare the team. We have a long journey ahead."

Meanwhile, within the seemingly impenetrable walls of the monastery, Brother Spinosa was absorbed in silent prayer. As serene as he appeared, he was not oblivious to the impending threat.

Spinosa was prepared for Pelham's attack. The documents they had left to be discovered were a diversion, leading Pelham's team into a labyrinthine chase away from the real sanctuary. The monastery's true location was known only to the highest-ranking members of the order and was never written down.

As Spinosa concluded his prayers, he felt a wave of tranquility wash over him. The path ahead was fraught with danger, but he was prepared. For the truth, for justice, they would stand strong against the brewing storm.

CHAPTER
TWENTY-FIVE

T he dappled morning light did little to quell the chill in the air as Lord Pelham, Trask, and a meticulously selected team of operatives disembarked from the helicopters. They found themselves on a remote mountain ridge, a wilderness of rugged cliffs and dense woodland stretching before them.

The documents had led them here, and if they were to be believed, somewhere amid this wilderness lay the elusive sanctuary of the Fellowship of the True Faith. Pelham's eyes scanned the landscape, the vast expanse seeming both threatening and exciting at the same time.

"Prepare for reconnaissance," Lord Pelham commanded with an air of authority, his hardened gaze unflinching as he studied the treacherous, rugged landscape. An intricate dance ensued as teams radiated out from the central point, spread thin across the wild terrain like fingers splayed out on a hand. Maintaining steady, crackling radio contact, they used state-of-the-art

imaging equipment and cutting-edge detection technology to systematically survey and map out the vast,
inhospitable area.

Their every moment was steeped in the relentless
ticking away of time. Hours slipped seamlessly into
days, the sun rose and fell in a fiery display, casting long,
undulating shadows that danced across the uneven
ground. Each new revelation they unearthed only led to
another dead end, another crushing disappointment. The
initial buzz of anticipation that had electrified the air
gradually began to morph into a palpable sense of frus-
tration. Pelham could taste the bitter tang of it on his
tongue, but he refused to let it consume him.

All the while, Trask, the ever-vigilant coordinator of
the intensive search operation, found a coil of unease
slowly unfurling within him. His brow creased under the
burden of his thoughts, worry lines deepening with
every fruitless hour that passed. Despite the cutting-edge
technology at their disposal, and the skilled team assembled, the elusive monastery continued to evade their
reach. Whispers of doubt began to slither into his mind,
chilling in their insinuation, but he swallowed them
down, daring not to voice them within earshot of Lord
Pelham.

Salvation came on the dawn of the third day. They
found a hidden valley cradled deep within the bosom of
the imposing mountains, its entrance artfully concealed
by a cascade of water that tumbled from a towering
height. It perfectly matched the cryptic descriptions that
had been extracted from the painstakingly decrypted
documents. Pelham, Trask, and the rest of their worn-out
team cautiously approached the entrance, hearts throb-

bing a percussive beat in their chests. Eager anticipation lit up their faces as they infiltrated the hidden crevice, creeping further into the belly of the beast.

However, as they delved deeper into the cavernous expanse, their buoyant excitement slowly began to wane, replaced by a creeping sense of dread that clung to their hearts.

There *were* signs of life—a deserted chapel, worn-out kneelers, a few faded frescoes—but no signs of the bustling community of brothers they had expected, no evidence of the valuable artifacts. It was as if the place had been abandoned for a long time.

"The monastery… it's a decoy," Trask finally admitted, the sinking realization mirrored in Pelham's stormy eyes. The dreaded truth descended upon them—they had been outwitted. The fury that came over Pelham was incendiary.

"They think they can make a fool of me?" Pelham's voice echoed ominously in the desolate chapel. "No! This ends now."

But even as he rallied his team, mustering them to continue the search in what now seemed an impossible quest, Pelham couldn't quell the seething anger within him. Outsmarted and outplayed, they had been led astray, and the real monastery remained a mystery. But he was far from admitting defeat. His dark quest, it seemed, had only just begun.

GIVEN Felix Bauer's role as a member of the Swiss Guard, his duties typically revolved around the security of

Vatican City and, most notably, the pope. Yet, the Swiss Guard also performs functions of diplomacy and public relations, their iconic uniforms serving as a visual representation of the Vatican's historic traditions.

In light of recent events—growing tensions within the Church, rumors of secret plots, and mounting public scrutiny—the Vatican decided to engage more directly with various religious communities in Italy, aiming to foster closer relationships and strengthen the Church's public image.

Cardinal Bennett Dreyfus was a master at the delicate dance of Vatican politics. With the savvy of a seasoned player, he operated in the shadowed corners of Church power. For his latest ploy, he turned his attention to Felix Bauer.

Bauer, with his disciplined demeanor and unwavering loyalty, was an ideal piece on Dreyfus's chessboard of influence. He was perfect for a mission that required absolute trust and discretion. Dreyfus knew the monastery of the Fellowship of the True Faith held crucial answers they needed, and he required a trusted agent to find it.

Formulating a plan under the guise of diplomacy, Dreyfus proposed an assignment for Bauer—to foster relations with the Convent of Santa Cecilia. This assignment was not about the religious artifacts at the Convent, but to probe information concerning the elusive monastery's whereabouts, under the pretext of diplomatic duties.

Seated within the sanctum of his office, Dreyfus, with meticulous care, crafted his proposal. He emphasized the diplomatic nature of the assignment when presenting it to the Swiss Guard's Commandant. He spoke of strengthening Vatican-convent relations, the good it would do for the Guard's reputation, and the residual benefits for the Church.

Convinced by Dreyfus's cogent argument, the commandant gave his approval. Thus, Bauer was dispatched to Santa Cecilia, under the guise of a diplomatic envoy but with a hidden mission. From his vantage point within the grand edifice of the Vatican, Dreyfus watched his chess pieces move. The game was on, and the stakes couldn't be higher.

IN THE HUSHED tranquility of the Convent of Santa Cecilia, nestled in the outskirts of Rome, Felix Bauer found a world that was a stark contrast to the guarded splendor of Vatican City. Here, among a community of nuns, he was a stranger to their faith-filled world.

His presence had been accepted as a gift, of sorts, from the Vatican, that of a Swiss Guard to further strengthen their relationship with Vatican City. They had welcomed his presence and given him the latitude to see their daily functions without hesitation. His assignment here was meant to be a brief interlude, a cover for his other, less holy, duties. Yet, as he observed the sisters in their daily activities—prayer, study, service—he began to witness a profound sincerity that sparked a curiosity within him.

One evening, Bauer found himself in the convent's chapel, a simple yet serene space filled with an aura of reverence. A group of nuns, young and old, sat in a semicircle, engrossed in a discussion led by Sister Lucia, an elderly nun with a countenance radiating wisdom and kindness.

Their topic of conversation wasn't theological doctrine or scriptural interpretation, but rather an exploration of their roles within the Church and society at large. It was a discourse on leadership, servitude, and most importantly, faith.

Each voice carried a story. Sister Gabriella, a younger nun, spoke passionately about her work with the homeless, her words pulsing with a profound compassion that moved Bauer. Sister Amelia, blind and nearing her eighties, recited poetry that she composed, offering wisdom with a quiet, lyrical grace that held the room in silent awe.

Sister Lucia, listening to each nun attentively, nodded encouragingly. Then, she spoke. Her voice, gentle yet firm, held a quality that immediately drew Bauer in.

"We, as women of the Church, often find ourselves overshadowed," she began. "Our voices are softer in the symphony of the Church's leadership. But that does not make us any less integral."

Her words resonated around the room, met with nods of agreement. "We may not wear the papal vestments, or command the Swiss Guard," she nodded with a small smile to Bauer, "but we shepherd in our own ways. We lead by example, by compassion, by service."

"By faith," chimed in Sister Gabriella, her eyes gleaming with conviction.

Bauer, a silent observer in the sea of soft murmurs and fervent whispers, found himself deeply moved. Standing at the threshold of the room, he felt the invisible currents of warmth and devotion that flowed between the nuns as they conducted their meeting. This was a far cry from the corridors of power he was accustomed to, with their cold marble floors and walls echoing with political intrigue and machinations. Yet, there was a palpable sense of leadership in this room—a leadership not asserted through dominance, manipulation, or coercion, but through love, service, and faith.

The nuns, humble in their attire but majestic in their poise, discussed their duties with a genuine concern for the wellbeing of others. There were no power plays here, no hidden agendas or self-serving ambitions. Instead, there was empathy, compassion, and an unbreakable bond that transcended their individual selves.

As the meeting adjourned, the sisters rose, their voices mingling in soft laughter and shared camaraderie. Their faces, marked by lines of wisdom and kindness, glowed with an inner light as they exchanged words of encouragement and gentle teasing. They were not just a community, Bauer realized, but a sisterhood—a family bound by shared faith, purpose, and an unwavering commitment to the greater good.

In the quiet that followed, Felix Bauer was left alone with his thoughts. The chapel, filled with the lingering echoes of devotion, seemed to envelop him in a serene embrace. He thought about his duties, his alliances, and the path he had chosen—a path marked by loyalty to powerful figures like Cardinal Dreyfus and Lord Pelham, men who wielded influence like a sword.

He thought about the words shared in the room, the sincerity of the nuns' faith, and their quiet yet impactful leadership. The contrast was striking, and it cut through his previously unshakable convictions. The political games he had played, the compromises he had made— they all seemed to pale in comparison to the purity of purpose he had witnessed among the sisters.

In the silence of the chapel, amidst the shadows of the evening, a seed of doubt was planted in Bauer's mind. His path, once so clearly defined, now seemed riddled with complexities he had not considered before. The ethical lines that had once appeared so distinct were blurring, and questions he had never dared to ask began to surface.

In the quiet leadership of the nuns, he had witnessed a testament to the strength of faith, a strength undiminished by gender or status. He found himself questioning the motives of Cardinal Dreyfus and Lord Pelham, his allegiance to their cause wavering in the face of this newfound perspective. A nagging voice within him began to question whether his loyalty had been misplaced, whether the goals he had pursued were truly noble, or whether he had been a pawn in a game he did not fully understand.

As the last rays of the sun filtered through the stained glass windows, casting a kaleidoscope of colors across the room, Bauer knew that he had reached a crossroads. The quiet conviction of the nuns had awakened something within him, something that called for reflection, reassessment, and perhaps, a new direction.

In the tranquility of that sacred space, Bauer found himself at the beginning of a profound personal journey —a journey toward understanding, integrity, and perhaps redemption. His mind, once closed and resolute, had been opened by the gentle strength of the sisters, and the path ahead, though uncertain, beckoned with the promise of truth and authenticity.

As the moon bathed the chapel in a soft glow, a Swiss Guard began to grapple with his convictions. He had come to Santa Cecilia to maintain a façade. But was he to leave with a stirring truth, one that could alter the course of his journey?

TWENTY-SIX

"Are we absolutely certain about this match?" Detective Inspector Grace Dempsey questioned Constable Leech, as she held out the report on the medallion that had been found on the body of Reverend Andrews.

"As certain as we can be, Inspector," Leech replied. "It's a perfect match for Karl Dengler."

Yet, something wasn't adding up for Dempsey. Since receiving the report a few days earlier, Dempsey had ordered considerable research into Karl's background which came out with a clean and exemplary profile on the decorated Swiss Guard. Karl had claimed to have found the medallion, yes, but he insisted he never touched it. And from what she knew of him, he seemed like the type to understand the importance of not contaminating evidence. Why would his fingerprint be on the medallion?

Picking up her desk phone, Dempsey called Karl in Rome.

Across the continent in Vatican City, Karl Dengler sat in stunned silence as Dempsey relayed the information to him. He could barely comprehend what he was hearing. His fingerprint on the medallion? But he had been so careful not to touch it!

"I promise you, Inspector Dempsey, I did not touch that medallion. Someone's trying to frame me," Karl protested, a mixture of anxiety and disbelief seeping into his voice. His words echoed in the silence of his Vatican City barracks, filling the room with an ominous sense of dread. He felt as though he was standing at the edge of a precipice, looking into an abyss of unfathomable depth and uncertainty.

A solitary bead of sweat trickled down his forehead as he clutched the phone tighter, his knuckles turning a ghostly white. His mind was in overdrive, reeling from the revelation. He had been meticulous, careful not to taint any evidence. Yet, his fingerprint had somehow found its way onto the medallion, an undeniable testament to his supposed guilt.

Back in Dorset, DI Dempsey was deep in thought, her fingers steepled in front of her, her gaze intense and probing. Karl's claim of being framed was not far-fetched. In her career, she had come across convoluted plots of deception and betrayal, instances where the innocent were made scapegoats, and the real culprits hid behind the veil of innocence.

"Alright, Karl," she replied, her voice steady and authoritative, yet holding a tinge of understanding. "We will look into this possibility. But you need to start from the beginning and recount every single detail. Anything might be of importance."

As Dempsey issued her directive, she knew she was

setting into motion a detailed and exhaustive investigation. It wasn't going to be easy. With the distance, involvement of different countries, and legal complications, they were traversing through murky waters, but the pursuit of truth was never meant to be easy.

Seated across the digital divide, Karl exhaled slowly. His mind rewound to the day he had found the medallion, the day that had marked the beginning of this bizarre and perilous journey. He recalled his discovery of the medallion, his not having even met Reverend Andrews before he died, and the recent individuals he had come into contact with. Every memory, every conversation, every seemingly insignificant detail was now under the scanner, holding potential clues to his innocence.

Across the miles, Dempsey listened attentively, her trained ears picking up the minutest of details, her mind working overtime to piece together the complex puzzle. She meticulously made notes, cross-referencing facts, and drawing possible connections. Every piece of information Karl offered, especially their being chased and shot at in Rome, was a potential lead in the elaborate labyrinth they found themselves in, a labyrinth they had to navigate meticulously to reach the truth.

As Karl relayed his interactions, one detail suddenly leapt out at Dempsey. He mentioned a certain ill-natured gentleman, a prominent figure Michael and Hana had encountered at Sherborne Abbey. A British aristocrat known as Lord Pelham.

"Wait," Dempsey interjected suddenly, her eyes flicking to the file Constable Leech had compiled on Dengler. She skimmed through the report until she found what she was looking for. "You said you met Lord Pelham at the abbey?"

"Well," Karl affirmed, "I didn't meet him personally, no. But he seemed... keen on the abbey's relics, as Michael mentioned it."

Dempsey felt a chill. Lord Pelham was known to her, of course, not only for his wealth and status but also for his vast network of connections. There were rumors of his involvement in various underhanded dealings, including tech-based crimes, but nothing had been substantiated. Yet, his sudden interest in the relics and his crossing paths with Karl's friends couldn't be mere coincidence.

She quickly added a note to delve deeper into Lord Pelham's activities, particularly those connected to advanced technology and cybercrime. It was possible that he had the means and knowledge to fake fingerprints. Dempsey braced herself for what could be a dangerous game of power, deceit, and tech-savvy crime. If Lord Pelham or his operatives were involved, it would take all her investigative skill to tie them to this crime.

CHAPTER
TWENTY-SEVEN

In the heart of Rome, under the moonlit façade of the majestic St. Peter's Basilica, a clandestine meeting was set to take place. Father Michael Dominic and Hana Sinclair, bathed in the silvery hues of the night, were standing in the middle of St. Peter's Square. The towering obelisk and encircling colonnades, usually teeming with life, now bore silent witness to their secret rendezvous. They had received an enigmatic message earlier in the day, instructing them to appear here at this late hour. Despite the risks and uncertainties, they had decided to come, their apprehension shadowed by a more powerful force—the thirst for truth.

From the spectral labyrinth of darkness, a solitary figure slowly emerged. It was Felix Bauer, the Swiss Guard, his vividly hued uniform standing out starkly in the monochromatic night. His usually stern visage was softened with remorse, anxiety etched into his rigidly set jawline.

"Father Michael, Signorina Sinclair," he greeted, his

voice carrying the weight of an unspoken apology. "I believe we have much to discuss."

Father Michael, surprised yet composed, replied with a curt nod, "Felix, you're the last person we expected to see tonight."

Felix Bauer swallowed, his Adam's apple bobbing visibly under the moonlight. "I'm afraid I've been led astray," he confessed, his voice strained. "I've made a terrible mistake."

A hushed silence fell over the trio, only the soft whistle of the cool night breeze filling the air. Bauer then began to unravel a tale of deception and betrayal. He recounted his recruitment by Cardinal Dreyfus and Lord Pelham, the enticing promises of higher stature, and his role in their sinister plans—including chasing and shooting at Karl's Jeep through the streets of Rome in a red VW sedan.

His words painted a vivid picture of his inner turmoil and eventual awakening. The turning point came in the shape of his recent assignment, a humble community of nuns who showed him the value of a woman's perspective in the Church. His realizations were like the pealing of cathedral bells, ringing through his conscience, growing louder until they drowned out the manipulative whispers of Pelham and Dreyfus.

"I couldn't just stand by," Bauer admitted, his gaze lowered. "Not after I came to understand the grave error of my ways."

Father Michael exhaled slowly, his priestly instincts taking over. "Felix, confession is the first step towards repentance," he said, his voice gentle but firm. "Your willingness to rectify your wrongs is commendable."

All eyes now fell on Hana Sinclair. Bauer shifted

nervously, awaiting her verdict. "I want to make it right," he implored, his sincerity resonating in his tone.

Hana looked deep into Bauer's eyes, a moment's contemplation reflecting in her own before she finally spoke. "To bring about change, we need allies, not adversaries. We accept your help, Felix."

With Bauer's defection, they gained an invaluable asset. His unique vantage point and access to the inner workings of their enemies' camp offered them an opportunity to anticipate Dreyfus's and Pelham's next moves. Bauer became their guide through the treacherous labyrinth that their enemies had laid before them. Together, they vowed to safeguard the invaluable relics —the Pope Joan diary and the Gospel of St. Salome—and support Pope Ignatius in his efforts for progressive reform.

With their newfound ally and a reinvigorated sense of purpose, Father Michael and Hana now stood poised on the cusp of a decisive phase of their mission. With every step, they were inching closer to exposing the truth and, in the process, turning the tables on Lord Pelham. The journey ahead was fraught with dangers, but the hope of a more inclusive Church fueled their resolve. As the moon continued to shine upon St. Peter's Square, the trio quietly dispersed, each carrying with them a piece of the unfolding saga and the burden of their shared responsibility.

~

SOME DAYS LATER, before dawn broke over Vatican City, Felix Bauer stood alone in the midst of the ethereal quiet. His mind, however, was anything but calm, buzzing with information that could unravel one of the most powerful figures in the English aristocracy. His allegiance to the truth, to Michael and Hana, and ultimately to the sanctity of the Church, had pushed him into an unfamiliar terrain.

Clad in his distinctive Renaissance-era uniform, Bauer began his day with a vigilant patrol around Vatican City, maintaining the meticulous façade of his regular duties. But underneath the surface, he was on a covert mission, a mission that transcended his duty as a Swiss Guard.

Bauer made a detour towards the Vatican Library, armed with an unassuming name from the network of Pelham's transactions—an ostensibly insignificant tech firm. With a quick word to the head librarian, an old acquaintance, he was given access to the library's comprehensive archives as well as its deep-diving internet resources.

Hours passed, and the sunlight streaming through the ornate windows shifted from a soft morning glow to a harsh afternoon glare. With a fervor akin to a detective's, Bauer combed through files and records until he unearthed a clandestine paper trail leading directly from Lord Pelham to the obscure tech company, with transactions that reeked of suspicion.

Back in his quarters in the Swiss Guard barracks, with the newfound evidence stashed securely, Bauer called Inspector Dempsey back in Dorset.

"Inspector, this is Corporal Felix Bauer," he said, his voice steady over the line. After explaining who he was and his former alliance with Lord Pelham—and his turn of face in view of the circumstances—he proceeded. "I've found something. From what Michael and Hana told me, it may just be the link you've been searching for."

As he relayed the information, there was silence on the other end, before Dempsey's voice reflected a tangible sense of anticipation. "Corporal Bauer, if this is what I think it is, you may have just handed us the evidence we need."

As he ended the call, Bauer looked out over Vatican City, his heart pounding. He was not just a Swiss Guard now; he had become a vital player in this intricate game of truth and deception, taking them one step closer to exposing Lord Pelham's devious machinations.

CHAPTER

TWENTY-EIGHT

I n the heart of Vatican City the next day, cloaked in the quiet sanctity of a secluded chapel, Felix Bauer sat hunched on a pew, fingers clutching a silver rosary, his heart pounding with an intensity that rivaled the echoing toll of the distant cathedral bell. He was not alone.

The last of the lingering daylight filtered through the stained glass windows, casting kaleidoscopic patterns on the cold marble floor. At the entrance of the chapel, two figures materialized. Karl and Lukas, the fellow countrymen he'd drifted apart from, stood silhouetted in the dim light.

"Felix," Karl called out, his usually jovial voice strained with an undertone of worry. The lack of the usual honorifics did not escape Bauer's notice. Lukas, usually the more reticent of the two, maintained a heavy silence as they cautiously approached the pew where Bauer sat.

"I owe you an explanation," Bauer began, his voice

echoing in the cavernous expanse of the chapel. He didn't meet their eyes; instead, he focused on the worn threads of the rosary entwined in his fingers.

As he unfurled his tale, his confessions filled the sacred air of the chapel. He revealed his manipulative recruitment by Cardinal Dreyfus and Lord Pelham, the allure of prestige that he'd fallen prey to, and his involvement in their insidious plans. The words left his lips in a torrent, the remorse apparent in every syllable.

The silence that followed Bauer's confession was deafening. Karl and Lukas exchanged uneasy glances. The Felix they'd known, the man who'd stood by their side in countless trials, the man they'd called a friend, was caught in a whirlwind of deceit.

Bauer finally mustered the courage to look up at his friends. Their faces were a mask of mixed emotions—betrayal, shock, but more than anything, sadness.

"I'm so sorry," Bauer whispered, his voice barely a shadow of its usual firmness. The heartfelt admission hung in the air like a confession before an altar. "I have been led astray, blinded by false promises."

Karl was the first to break the silence, his jovial nature subdued as he stepped forward. "Felix, we always saw you as a man of honor, a man of integrity. This… it's hard to accept."

"I know," Bauer replied, his voice choked with emotion. "And I understand if you can't forgive me. I just… I just wanted you to know the truth."

Silence descended upon the chapel once again, broken only by the faint whisper of a prayer from a distant corridor. Bauer braced himself for rejection, the possibility of losing his friends a heavy weight on his heart.

But Lukas, always the silent observer, finally stepped forward. "Felix," he started, his usually soft voice bearing a new hardness. "We've known each other for a long time. We've seen the best and worst of each other. Your mistake... it's a part of you, but it's not all of you."

He met Bauer's surprised gaze, a small, warm smile playing on his lips. "We all make mistakes, Felix. What matters is that you've owned up to yours and you're trying to make amends."

Karl nodded in agreement. "And we're going to help you do that," he affirmed, his usual joviality returning. "We're in this together, like always."

In the fading light of the chapel, Felix Bauer found his redemption—not just in his confession, but in the unwavering friendship of Karl and Lukas. It was a moment of painful revelation, of sincere confession, and ultimately, of profound forgiveness. Their shared faith, and the unshakeable bond of their friendship, promised a new dawn, a chance to right the wrongs, and a path towards redemption.

CHAPTER
TWENTY-NINE

The Dorset police department wasn't just known for its efficiency but also for its progressive approach to law enforcement. One such leap forward was their dedicated digital forensics unit, headed by a young but remarkably talented expert, Neil Simmons. Inspector Dempsey, having laid out her suspicions about Lord Pelham and the fingerprint, approached Simmons to seek his expertise in tracking the technological breadcrumbs.

"Neil, I have a case that could use your particular set of skills," Dempsey started, laying the file on his cluttered desk, with the complex network of Lord Pelham's connections and the suspicion of digitally manipulated fingerprints clearly laid out.

Simmons skimmed through the file, his interest piqued. He had dealt with fraud, theft, and even cyber-terrorism, but a potential case of faked fingerprints was uncharted territory. It was a challenge he was ready to tackle.

"All right, Inspector. I'll get started right away," he said, already firing up his array of systems and beginning the process.

The first order of business was to isolate the original fingerprint file from the forensics. Each digital file carries with it a trace of metadata—timestamps, locations, and even details about the software used to create it. If this print was indeed tampered with, the metadata was likely tampered with as well.

Like a master artisan, Neil Simmons immersed himself in the vast digital landscape that spanned before him. Day by day, hour by hour, he wrestled with the daunting complexities of the digital puzzle that lay before him. His computer screen was a canvas of endless code, strings of numbers, and symbols that were seemingly indecipherable to the untrained eye. But to Neil, it was a language he had mastered over the years.

Fueled by countless cups of black coffee and the thrill of the chase, he hunched over his desk, his fingers dancing over the keyboard as he set to work writing advanced algorithms. These were tailored to sift through the mountains of metadata, to isolate the outliers, the subtle digital footprints left behind in the wake of manipulation.

This work was less about the brute force of computing power and more about the finesse of understanding patterns, of discerning the tell-tale signatures of artificial tampering amid the organic flow of genuine data. It was a daunting challenge, akin to finding a needle in a cyber haystack. Each lead he followed felt like threading a path through a dense jungle, with potential clues hidden beneath layers of complex coding language.

As he wove his way through the labyrinth, he began uncovering fragments of the larger picture. An anomalous timestamp here, an inconsistent location tag there. Bit by bit, byte by byte, a trail began to emerge, faint but discernible. Each breakthrough was a small victory, a spark of clarity in the overwhelming chaos of the digital maze.

By marrying his in-depth knowledge of digital forensics with his remarkable knack for pattern recognition, Neil was slowly but surely tracing the digital breadcrumbs back to their origin. The mystery was far from solved, but the veil of uncertainty was beginning to lift. The picture, once hazy and distorted, was becoming increasingly sharper, gradually revealing the hidden truth.

The breakthrough came on the fourth day. A line of code pointed towards a specific software—an advanced biometrics manipulation tool only a handful of companies worldwide had the expertise and resources to develop.

Cross-referencing this information with Inspector Dempsey's report on Lord Pelham's financial transactions, Neil found a sizable payment from Pelham to a tech company renowned for such advanced software. The company was discreet, known to work only with exclusive clients.

Armed with this information, Neil met Dempsey in her office. "We've got him," he said, placing the evidence in front of her. "Or at least, we've got a substantial lead. Lord Pelham financed a company that specializes in the very technology I can ascertain with high certainty was used to fake the fingerprint."

Dempsey couldn't suppress a triumphant smile. The

labyrinth was beginning to unravel, and every sign was pointing towards Lord Pelham. "Excellent work, Neil. Let's keep digging. It's time we shed light on Lord Pelham's activities and bring justice for Reverend Andrews."

With a renewed surge of determination, they were now one step closer to unmasking the puppeteer behind the scenes.

ARMED with the digital forensics report that had unearthed Lord Pelham's payment to the tech company specializing in advanced biometrics manipulation, DI Grace Dempsey felt a rising tide of anticipation. This was the break they needed, the lead that could finally shed light on the dark machinations behind Reverend Andrews's murder and Karl's framing.

"Neil, this is good. But we need to tread carefully," Dempsey said, her eyes scanning the report once more. "We need to connect Pelham directly to the software and this crime. I want you to dive into the tech company's digital footprint. Any emails, internal memos, transactions that connect the software to Pelham and our case. Can you do it?"

Neil nodded with a determined glint in his eyes. "I'm on it, Inspector."

Meanwhile, Dempsey had another angle to play. She approached Judge Harriet Styles, a stern but fair magistrate known for her absolute commitment to justice. Laying out the intricate web of evidence, she made a case for a search warrant of Lord Pelham's estates and assets.

"Your Honor," she stated with conviction, "I believe Lord Pelham purchased unique software capable of fabricating biometrics. I have strong reason to believe that this software was used to forge Karl Dengler's fingerprint on the medallion found on Reverend Andrews's body. I request a search warrant to inspect Lord Pelham's properties and digital assets for any evidence of this software or any other evidence linked to Reverend Andrews's murder."

Judge Styles listened attentively, her sharp gaze never wavering from Dempsey's as the Inspector laid out her case against Lord Pelham. She was renowned in judicial circles for her insightful understanding of the law, her unyielding pursuit of justice, and her ability to dissect even the most complicated arguments with a surgeon's precision. Her chambers filled with an anticipatory silence as she considered Dempsey's request.

After a thoughtful pause, she finally spoke, her voice carrying the weight of her office. "Inspector Dempsey, the allegations you're making are grave, with wide-ranging repercussions. And the person you're accusing is no common criminal. Lord Pelham is a man of significant influence and resources."

She let the reality of the situation sink in before continuing. "However, the pursuit of justice is the very foundation of our profession. If these accusations hold merit, it's our duty to expose the truth, no matter who the guilty party is."

With that, she agreed to issue the search warrant, but her next words were a pointed reminder of the delicate path they were treading. "Dempsey, you're stepping on some powerful toes. Make sure your evidence is unimpeachable. You need to build a case that can stand against the inevitable counterblow."

Back at the station, the search warrant in hand felt

like a weighty responsibility. Holding the thin piece of paper, Inspector Dempsey felt the pulse of expectation. It was a powerful tool, the key to unlocking the secrets Lord Pelham might be hiding.

She felt the gravity of their task, the fine line they had to tread between diligence and discretion. Lord Pelham's properties needed to be searched meticulously. Every file, every document, every device could potentially hold the key to confirming Pelham's guilt.

This was not just about uncovering a heinous crime but also about preserving the sanctity of their pursuit of justice. Any misstep, any indiscretion could jeopardize the case and provide Lord Pelham with an escape route. They had a lead, a solid one at that, and they had to ensure they followed it to the end, upholding the principles they stood for in their quest for truth.

She assembled her team in the squad room, a diverse group of dedicated officers who had proven their mettle time and again. There was a shifting energy in the room, a mix of anticipation and determination, as they prepared for the crucial task ahead.

"We need to act swiftly and discretely," Dempsey stressed, eyeing each of her officers in turn. "Lord Pelham's properties are extensive, but they must be combed thoroughly. We're looking for anything that connects him to the tech company or to Reverend Andrews. Also, keep an eye out for any evidence of advanced tech and biometric software."

Dempsey called upon Police Constable Jonathan Miller, a veteran with years of experience in such intricate searches. "Miller, I need your best men on this. We're searching all of Pelham's properties. We're looking for any signs of advanced tech, paperwork linking him to the tech company, anything related to Reverend Andrews, or anything that stands out as suspicious."

As Miller's team set off to comb through Pelham's properties, Neil Simmons continued his digital exploration. The task was monumental, but they had one lead, one loose thread that, if pulled right, could unravel Lord Pelham's carefully woven tapestry of deceit.

As the net tightened around Lord Pelham, Dempsey felt the weight of their responsibility. They weren't just seeking justice for Reverend Andrews; they were fighting to clear an innocent man's name. There was no room for mistakes, no opportunity for oversights. Every move had to be calculated, every piece of evidence indisputable. The truth was within their grasp, and they were determined to bring it to light.

THIRTY

With warrant in hand, Dempsey's team descended upon Lord Pelham's extensive estates like a silent storm. They moved methodically through grand halls, secreted offices, and lavish living spaces, their eyes sharply tuned to any irregularities. The task was monumental, and they worked in hushed concentration, aware of the high stakes.

Meanwhile, back at the station, Neil Simmons burrowed deep into the complex digital pathways of the tech company's systems, inching closer to connecting Pelham to the purchase of the biometric manipulation software.

In the opulence of one of Pelham's more secluded home offices, PC Jonathan Miller found himself facing a grandiose oil painting of a hunting scene. There was an innate intuition, a detective's sixth sense that urged him to take a closer look. Years in the force had taught him that guilty secrets often hid behind a veneer of extravagance.

Pulled by this gut instinct, Miller examined the artwork, running his gloved fingers along the gilded frame, his eyes tracing the masterfully painted scene of hounds and hunters. It was then he noticed a slight irregularity, a tiny hinge peeking out from behind the heavy, gold frame. With a surge of adrenaline, he moved the painting to reveal a concealed safe, elegantly hidden within the wall.

The safe was a fortress in itself, sporting a state-of-the-art digital lock. Calling in their tech specialist from the van stationed discreetly outside the mansion, the team worked to crack the code, the tension in the room tangible.

Finally, after several tense minutes, the lock gave way with a quiet beep, and the safe door swung open to reveal a stack of meticulously filed documents. They were invoices, contracts, and emails, all linked to a tech firm with an innocuously bland name—"Beryl Innovations."

To an unsuspecting eye, Beryl Innovations might appear as just another player in the tech industry. But Dempsey's team had already uncovered its dark side. The company, as Neil had discovered, was a front for a group specializing in advanced biometric manipulation software. They were the ones behind the technology capable of creating perfect replicas of fingerprints, placing them seamlessly on objects of choice.

Each piece of paper Miller held was a damning link in the chain tying Lord Pelham to the fabricated fingerprint found on the OPG medallion. Each transaction with Beryl Innovations was a testament to a well-planned, devious plot to frame Karl Dengler for a murder he didn't commit. And right at the center of this web of deceit was Lord Pelham.

The documents were carefully collected, sealed in evidence bags to be further examined by their forensics team. As PC Miller emerged from the secluded office, the cache of hidden documents in tow, there was a palpable shift in the atmosphere. They were one step closer to nailing the puppeteer orchestrating this dangerous game, one step closer to serving justice.

With the conclusive evidence in hand, Dempsey felt a surge of grim satisfaction. Their tireless efforts had borne fruit, but the most challenging part was yet to come—the arrest of Lord Pelham.

LUCIUS PELHAM WAS in his private study in his London townhouse when Dempsey and her team arrived. His eyes widened in surprise and then narrowed in defiance as the inspector, her face impassive but her eyes steel-hard, showed him the arrest warrant.

"Lord Pelham, you are under arrest for the murder of Reverend Andrews and the framing of Karl Dengler," she declared, her voice echoing in the ornate study.

In a show of aristocratic indignation, Lord Pelham pushed back, "This is preposterous! I have done no such thing. You're ruining my reputation on baseless accusations!"

Dempsey stood her ground, an island of unyielding resolve amidst the storm of Lord Pelham's indignation. "We have evidence, Lord Pelham," she reiterated, her tone as steely as her gaze. "Documented transactions, digital trails... all leading back to a tech firm that specializes in biometric manipulation. A firm, it seems, that you have had multiple dealings with."

Her words filled the room, bouncing off the rich mahogany walls and the imposing bookcases lined with countless leather-bound volumes. They landed with the force of a gavel, echoing with the irrefutable truth they carried.

"Your fingerprints, Lord Pelham," she continued, the indictment building with each fact she laid bare. "Your financial fingerprints are clearly enough evidence to link you to the crime, enough to suggest you orchestrated the entire setup."

The accusations hung heavily in the air, their implications as palpable as the tension that coiled in the room. Lord Pelham's face drained of color, his mask of aristocratic nonchalance slipping to reveal a flicker of apprehension. However, his resolve, albeit shaken, didn't crumble. He was a man used to battling controversies, a seasoned player in the game of power and deception.

His gaze moved to the ornate side table, where a silver letter opener lay, glinting ominously under the overhead lights. It was a desperate instinct, a cornered animal's fight for survival. But Dempsey's team was ready.

Before he could so much as twitch, PC Miller, his senses honed by years in the field, had lunged forward, pinning Pelham's arms to his side in an unyielding grip. The sudden restraint startled Pelham, his eyes widening in surprise and dawning realization.

"You have the right to remain silent, Lord Pelham," PC Miller stated, his voice steady, echoing the familiar words of the legal caution used in such arrests in several countries. He continued the recitation, outlining

Pelham's rights even as the aristocrat struggled futilely against his grip.

Despite the fierce resistance, Lord Pelham was taken into custody, and a murmur of shock rippled across the country. As the news of his arrest spread, Detective Inspector Grace Dempsey felt a sense of somber accomplishment. This was a significant victory, but their work was far from over. Now, they had to ensure that Lord Pelham faced the full brunt of justice.

CHAPTER
THIRTY-ONE

P ope Ignatius sat in his wheelchair at the head of a long, ornate wooden table in the Vatican's Apostolic Palace. The dimly lit room echoed with whispers and murmurs, as a diverse assembly of cardinals, bishops, and theologians gathered to discuss the monumental changes proposed by His Holiness. The air was heavy with anticipation and tension, as they awaited the moment when the pope would unveil his decisions concerning the future of the Catholic Church.

It had been several weeks since Pope Ignatius had read the diary of Pope Joan and the Gospel of St. Salome, and the profound impact of these revelations weighed heavily on his heart. He had spent countless hours in prayer and contemplation, wrestling with the decision to challenge centuries of Church doctrine and tradition. Now, with the help of his trusted advisors, Pope Ignatius prepared to outline his vision for a more inclusive and egalitarian Church.

As the room fell silent, the pope began to speak in a

calm, measured voice. "My dear brothers and sisters in Christ, we are gathered here today to discuss matters of great importance to our Church and its faithful. You have now been given the privilege of reading two remarkable documents—the diary of Pope Joan and the Gospel of St. Salome. These artifacts have shed light on aspects of our faith that have been obscured and misrepresented throughout history. They have challenged us to reconsider our understanding of the role of women in the Church and, by extension, the prohibition against priests marrying."

Cardinal Mendez, a staunch conservative and one of the pope's most vocal critics, interrupted the pontiff's remarks. "Your Holiness, I must protest. The authenticity of these documents is still in question, and we cannot simply abandon centuries of tradition based on dubious evidence."

Pope Ignatius raised a hand to silence the cardinal. "I appreciate your concerns, Cardinal Mendez, but I have prayed on this matter and consulted with experts in theology, history, and archaeology. The Holy Spirit has guided me to a deep conviction that these documents are genuine and that their message is of vital importance to the Church."

The pope paused for a moment, allowing his words to sink in. "After much reflection, I have decided to issue an Apostolic Constitution outlining the Church's commitment to the recognition and inclusion of women in all aspects of our faith. Furthermore, I am also preparing to make a constitutional statement removing the prohibition against priests marrying. I believe these changes are essential to the future of our Church, and that they are in keeping with the teachings of Christ."

A mixture of surprise, shock, and murmurs filled the room. Some of the assembled clergy nodded in agreement, while others exchanged skeptical glances.

Sister Elaine Thompson, one of the few female religious leaders in attendance, spoke up in support of the pope's proposal. "Your Holiness, I am deeply grateful for your willingness to recognize the contributions of women in the Church and to promote their inclusion in leadership roles. This is a much-needed step toward healing and unity within our faith community."

Others, like Archbishop Giuseppe Bellini, were more cautious in their response. "Your Holiness, while I understand the need for change and progress, I worry that these proposals may be too radical and could lead to division and strife within the Church. How can we ensure that our congregation will accept these new teachings?"

Pope Ignatius nodded solemnly, acknowledging the archbishop's concerns. "I share your worries, Archbishop Bellini. That is why I have called this assembly of our Church's most esteemed minds. I need your wisdom, your guidance, and your support in this endeavor. Together, we must develop a comprehensive plan for implementing these changes in a way that fosters unity, understanding, and growth."

Over the next several hours, the room buzzed with passionate discussions and debates as the assembly worked to develop a plan for implementing the pope's proposals. There were moments of heated disagreement, but also instances of profound understanding and empathy as the clergy grappled with the implications of these historic changes.

Pope Ignatius listened carefully to the concerns and

suggestions of his advisors, taking notes and asking questions to clarify their positions. It was important to him that everyone's voice was heard, regardless of whether they agreed with his decisions. He knew that the success of these reforms hinged on the support and cooperation of the entire Church.

As the meeting progressed, several key strategies emerged to guide the implementation of the pope's proposals. First and foremost, it was agreed that a comprehensive educational campaign would be necessary to help the faithful understand the theological and historical basis for these changes. Seminaries and theological institutions would be encouraged to revise their curricula to include the study of Pope Joan's diary and the Gospel of St. Salome, and a series of conferences and workshops would be organized to facilitate dialogue and debate among theologians, clergy, and laypeople.

Another important aspect of the plan involved the development of new pastoral guidelines and liturgical practices to promote the inclusion of women in the Church. This would involve reevaluating existing rules and traditions to identify and eliminate any barriers to gender equality. Additionally, the Church would establish a special commission to identify and promote qualified women for leadership positions within the Church hierarchy.

Finally, the assembly acknowledged that the decision to allow priests to marry would require significant adjustments to the Church's infrastructure and support systems. Committees would be formed to examine the financial, logistical, and pastoral implications of this change and to develop strategies for integrating married clergy into the existing Church framework.

GARY MCAVOY

As the meeting drew to a close, Pope Ignatius addressed the assembly once more. "My dear brothers and sisters, I am deeply grateful for your honesty, your dedication, and your willingness to engage in this difficult conversation. I know that the changes we have discussed today will not be easy, and that they will require courage, patience, and trust in the guidance of the Holy Spirit.

"But I also believe, with all my heart, that these changes are necessary if our Church is to remain faithful to the teachings of Christ and responsive to the needs of our world. As we embark on this journey together, let us remember the words of Proverbs 3:5-6, '*Trust in the Lord with all your heart and lean not on your own understanding; in all your ways submit to him, and he will make your paths straight.*' May these words guide us as we navigate through these challenging times, always seeking truth, unity, and the betterment of our faith."

Pope Ignatius offered a final blessing, and the assembly dispersed to begin the challenging but essential work of implementing the historic changes that would reshape the Catholic Church for generations to come.

CHAPTER

THIRTY-TWO

T he room, rich with the scent of centuries-old vellum and the solemn weight of knowledge, lay under an almost palpable silence as Pope Ignatius paused, his eyes shifting meaningfully from the faces of Michael and Hana to the vibrantly colored image of Pope Joan that dominated the room. This wasn't just any depiction. It was an original, an authentic rendition that had spent centuries tucked away in obscurity, languishing in the labyrinthine depths of the Vatican Museum. Its true significance had been misinterpreted, its monumental historical value overlooked in an era when the possibility of a female Pope was unthinkable.

The image was of a figure of unmistakable authority. Clothed in the papal white, she held the staff of St. Peter in one hand and the Holy Bible in the other. Her gaze was cast downward, serene yet firm, an expression of humility coupled with resolute strength. For years, this enigmatic figure had been considered merely a symbolic representation of the Church or some lost saint. The suggestion that it might depict a female Pope was dismissed as heretical fantasy. Yet, here she was, Pope Joan, her visage resurrected from the oblivion of ignorance and misinterpretation.

"Joan," Ignatius said, the echo of the name filling the room with a profound resonance. The sound hung in the air like a long-awaited sigh of relief, shattering the centuries-old veil of denial with its bold assertion. "She was a pope. Our pope.

"She led our Church," Ignatius continued, each word heavy with the gravitas of the revelation. "She guided our ancestors in faith, wielding the spiritual authority granted to the successor of Peter. She, like Peter, was a rock, a beacon of God's light in the world. She served with wisdom and grace, a testament to the divine in all of us, irrespective of our gender."

There was an inherent reverence in his voice as he spoke of Joan's memory, a memory that had been unjustly tarnished and concealed. "Her memory deserves to be honored, not buried," he asserted, his eyes meeting Michael's and Hana's in silent agreement. "For too long, the world has been denied the truth. Now, we must restore Joan to her rightful place in history, not as an apocryphal figure, but as a Pope who served her Church and her God with honor."

His voice softened as he added, "We owe it to her, to the generations of faithful who were denied the knowledge of her service, and to the future believers who deserve to know the full truth. We must correct the course of history, steer it away from denial and towards the shores of acceptance and acknowledgment. We must honor Pope Joan."

The revelation, momentous and profound, hung in

the air, creating a current of understanding that surged through the room. It was a commitment to truth, a pledge to challenge tradition if it meant restoring justice. The silence that followed wasn't merely the absence of noise, but a powerful testament to the gravity of the truth they were about to unearth. The path ahead was fraught with uncertainty and possible backlash, but the resolve in the room, hardened in the crucible of this historic moment, was ready to weather any storm.

THE APOSTOLIC PALACE hummed with a fervor of activity, echoing with the hurried footsteps of cardinals, the hushed whispers of secretaries, and the intermittent clicks and whirrs of media teams from around the world. Amidst the flurry, atop the grand balcony of his apartment, sat Pope Ignatius, frail yet resolute, ensconced in a wheelchair.

His aging hands, witnesses to countless prayers, were clasped gently in his lap, and his eyes, carrying the wisdom of his years, were closed in contemplative meditation. His body might have been succumbing to the passage of time, but his spirit remained undeterred. This was a gathering he had prepared for, a message he was duty-bound to deliver before his mortal journey reached its final destination.

His once strong and sturdy frame, now weak and trembling, held a gravitas that defied his physical frailty. The wheelchair did nothing to diminish his authority or the depth of reverence he commanded from the congregation below.

As he slowly opened his eyes, the throng of onlookers

fell silent. The papal apartment overlooked St. Peter's Square, offering a view of a sea of faces turned upward in anticipation. A thousand eyes, twinkling like the stars of a clear Roman night, were fixed upon the elderly pontiff. It was in this moment of profound silence that Pope Ignatius, weak in body but unyielding in spirit, prepared to reveal a truth long shrouded in the annals of the Church's history.

"Brothers and sisters, I stand before you today, not just as your Pope, but as your brother in faith," he started, his voice resonating with an undeniable warmth. "As servants of Christ, we are called to seek truth, even when it is uncomfortable, and stand for justice, even when it requires us to challenge the familiar and the traditional."

He paused, letting his words sink in, before he unveiled the monumental revelation. "In light of this duty, I bring you today a truth that has been obscured for too long. Our Church, our Holy See, once had a woman at its helm."

An audible gasp rippled through the crowd, the shockwave of his words echoing off the ancient stone buildings surrounding St. Peter's Square.

"Joan," he continued, the name carrying an undeniable weight. "She was a pope, chosen by the faithful, entrusted with the Keys of Heaven, and she served with grace, courage, and wisdom."

He raised his hand, silencing the murmur that began to rise. "We have found undeniable evidence that confirms her existence and her papacy. She guided our Church, shepherded our ancestors in faith, and served Christ in her own right."

His gaze swept over the crowd, his voice steady as he

addressed the unspoken questions, the underlying fears. "The recognition of Pope Joan should not challenge our faith; it enriches it. It demonstrates that the Holy Spirit can work through anyone, regardless of gender, to guide our Church."

"The legacy of Pope Joan," he concluded, "should no longer be obscured in the shadows of misunderstanding and ignorance. We honor her today as a true Successor of Peter and invite the world to remember her with the reverence she rightfully deserves."

As his aides pulled the wheelchair back, the silence was almost deafening before the crowd erupted into a cacophony of whispers and gasps, the impact of the revelation hitting like a thunderclap. Cameras flashed, reporters scrambled to broadcast the news, and the world watched, stunned, as history was rewritten. And in that moment, the Church stepped forward into a new era, one where truth, no matter how long hidden or how uncomfortable, held sway.

Nestled amidst the throng of faithful followers, a cluster of nuns from various orders bore witness to the momentous declaration. For these women, devoted servants of the Church, the words held a profound significance. They had given their lives to the service of God and His Church, often navigating a path rife with quiet trials and subtle dismissals. And now, they were witnessing a seismic shift in that narrative.

Sister Maria, an elderly nun with kind eyes, stood with her hands clasped together, her rosary beads wound tightly around her fingers. Tears welled in her eyes, not of sadness, but of relief and a deep, resonating joy. The struggle for recognition, for respect, seemed suddenly validated. She looked to her side, where a young novice, Sister Lucia, stared in awe at the Apostolic Palace. The younger nun's face was a mirror of shock, her eyes wide as saucers, her mouth slightly agape.

Whispers spread amongst the nuns, breathless exchanges of disbelief, wonder, and for some, vindication. Many hugged each other, their black and white habits merging into a symbol of unity. Some broke into quiet sobs, their tears absorbed by the soft fabric of their wimples. Others merely stood still, their faces turned skyward, their hands clasped in silent prayer.

A chorus of cheers began to swell, starting as a murmur before amplifying into a roar that echoed throughout the square. The nuns joined in, their voices joining the cacophony of jubilation. The Church, their Church, had taken a significant leap forward, opening its doors wider to acknowledge the role a woman had faithfully filled in its history.

In that moment, they were no longer merely observers; they were active participants in a historic shift that would shape the future of the Church they so loved and served. It was a moment etched into their hearts, one that would be retold in hushed tones within the quiet corridors of their convents and echo through the ages as a triumphant milestone in their spiritual journey.

CHAPTER
THIRTY-THREE

The sun was setting, casting long shadows across the chambers of Pope Ignatius, painting the room in hues of orange and gold. Despite his weakening body, the pope's eyes held an unquenchable flame, a determination that refused to bow to his failing health. The room around him held silent except for the rhythmic ticking of the ancient clock on the wall.

At his side was a small table, an oasis of order in the middle of medical paraphernalia that now commonly surrounded him no matter where he stationed himself. On the table lay two meticulously prepared documents —Apostolic Constitutions, the final edicts of his papacy. One was a decree on the empowerment of women in the Church; the other, an official sanction allowing priests to marry.

As his private secretary, Father Nick Bannon, gently handed him an ornate fountain pen, the pope glanced over the parchments, the weight of the moment resting heavily upon his frail shoulders. Each word, each sentence had been carefully crafted, embodying the culmination of his vision for a Church more inclusive, more open to change. These were not just documents. They were promises for a future that he would not live to see but believed in with every fiber of his being.

His eyes travelled over the preamble of the first Constitution, a declaration acknowledging the unsung women who had, for centuries, served the Church in the shadows. His signature on this parchment would bring them into the light, validating their contributions and paving the way for the enhanced participation in the Church's affairs for current and future women in the Church.

The second parchment held similar import. The bold script detailed a radical shift from centuries-old celibacy rules, allowing priests the freedom to marry. It was a change he had long contemplated, a change that would bring the priesthood closer to the everyday lives and challenges of their flock. At that moment, he thought of Michael, his son. This would alter his son's life significantly, if he chose that path.

Taking a deep breath, he gripped the pen, feeling the familiar coolness of its metal nib. A sense of tranquility washed over him, and with a steady hand, he signed his name on the documents, one after the other—Ignatius PP.

As he finished, he took a moment to gaze at his signatures, not as mere autographs but as imprints of hope, catalysts for change. With a sigh of satisfaction, he handed the quill back to his secretary, the two Constitutions signed and sealed, ready to be announced to the world.

"May these serve as the seeds for a new era in our

Church," Pope Ignatius whispered, a soft smile on his lips. He then leaned back onto his chair, closing his eyes, the light of his legacy burning brightly against the encroaching dusk.

Apostolic Constitution of the Supreme Pontiff Pope Ignatius
"De munere Mulierum in Ecclesia et agnitione Papae Joan"
On the Role of Women in the Church and the Acknowledgment of Pope Joan

To the Bishops, Priests, Deacons, Consecrated Persons, and the Lay Faithful Venerable Brothers and Sisters in Christ,

Ladies and gentlemen, dear brothers and sisters in Christ, esteemed members of the press, and all those joining us from around the world, I, Pope Ignatius, stand before you today as the humble servant of our Lord Jesus Christ and the Catholic Church. It is with great solemnity and a profound sense of responsibility that I address you on this historic occasion.

Over the centuries, the Catholic Church has been a source of guidance, solace, and inspiration to countless individuals. Our mission to serve and share the teachings of Christ has been unwavering. However, like any human institution, the Church has not been without its shortcomings. Today, we seek to acknowledge and learn from one such instance in our past.

For centuries, there has been a persistent legend

about Pope Joan, a woman who, disguised as a man, is said to have been elected Pope in the ninth century. Scholars have debated her existence, and the Church has largely remained silent on the matter. After thorough examination of historical records and recent discoveries, I must now acknowledge the truth: Pope Joan did exist, and she played a significant role in the Church's history.

Pope Joan's story is a testament to the courage, wisdom, and determination of countless women who, throughout the ages, have contributed to the life and mission of the Church. Her legacy is a reminder that the spirit of God moves within all of us, regardless of gender.

In light of this revelation, and as part of our ongoing commitment to social justice, it is my duty as the Bishop of Rome to further the cause of gender equality within our Church. Thus, I am announcing the following initiatives:

— Firstly, the establishment of a commission to reevaluate the role of women in the Church, with a focus on identifying ways to empower them and afford them equal opportunities in all aspects of Church life.

— Secondly, a commitment to ensuring that women are included in decision-making processes at all levels of the Church, both in the Vatican and in local parishes.

— And lastly, the promotion of theological education and leadership training for women, to foster a new generation of female theologians, scholars, and pastoral leaders.

In the spirit of Pope Joan, we must strive to break down the barriers that have prevented women from realizing their full potential within the Church. By embracing the gifts and talents of all members of our community, we will become stronger, more compassionate, and better equipped to carry out Christ's mission in the world.

Today, I ask for your prayers and support as we embark on this important journey. Let us walk together in the footsteps of Jesus Christ, guided by the Holy Spirit, and united in our mission to bring love, justice, and peace to our world.

Thank you, and may God bless each and every one of you.

Pope Ignatius PP.

~

Apostolic Constitution of the Supreme Pontiff Pope Ignatius

"DE SACRAMENTO S. MATRIMONII PRO SACERDOTIBUS": ON THE SACRAMENT OF HOLY MATRIMONY FOR PRIESTS

To the Bishops, Clergy, and Faithful of the Catholic Church

Venerable Brothers and Sisters in Christ,

With a heart full of hope and love for the Church, I, Pope Ignatius, born Enrico Petrini, address you today to solemnly declare a new understanding of the Sacrament of Holy Matrimony as it pertains to the priests of the Catholic Church.

Throughout the centuries, the Church has maintained the discipline of celibacy for priests in the Latin Rite, valuing the complete dedication of their lives to the service of God and His people. This practice has brought numerous spiritual benefits, enabling priests to focus entirely on their ministry and imitate the life of our Lord Jesus Christ.

However, in these modern times, we have witnessed the challenges faced by our beloved priests as they strive to meet the pastoral needs of their communities. It has become increasingly evident that the gift of marriage, a reflection of God's love for His Church, can also enrich the lives and ministries of our priests.

After much prayer and reflection, and in communion with the bishops and theologians, I have decided, by the authority vested in me as the Successor of Saint Peter and the Vicar of Christ on earth, to promulgate this Apostolic Constitution on the matter of the Sacrament of Holy Matrimony for priests in the Latin Rite.

Therefore, by my apostolic authority, I decree the following:

The Sacrament of Holy Matrimony, in its true essence and sanctity, shall be allowed for priests in the Latin Rite, who may now enter into the covenant of marriage with the understanding that their primary commitment remains to their priestly vocation and the service of God's people.

This change shall not diminish the value of celibacy or its spiritual significance but shall serve to recognize the diversity of gifts that the Holy Spirit bestows upon the Church, allowing priests the freedom to discern their unique path of service to God and His people.

As we embrace this new understanding of the Sacrament of Holy Matrimony for priests, I call upon the bishops, clergy, and faithful of the Catholic Church to support and pray for our priests as they embark on this journey of love, commitment, and service in the name of Christ and His Church.

Pope Ignatius PP.

CHAPTER

THIRTY-FOUR

As dusk settled over Vatican City, the muted rustle of sacred parchment echoed throughout the chambers of the Apostolic Palace. Within these venerable walls, Father Michael Dominic sat across from Pope Ignatius, a formidable figure despite his advancing age and ailing health.

They found themselves in the midst of a profound discussion, probing the depths of Church history, their conversation centered around the enigma of Pope Joan. Strewn across the ornate desk between them lay fragments of evidence—the diary and the gospel—silent testimonials of a legacy that dared to challenge the long-standing traditions of their faith.

With a sigh that seemed to carry the weight of centuries, Pope Ignatius broke their reverie. "You know, Michael," he began, the lines on his face deepening in the candlelight, "I've always been intrigued by one particular... artifact from our past."

The younger priest watched the pontiff's face, his curiosity piqued. "Your Holiness?"

"The Sedia Stercoraria," Pope Ignatius declared, his eyes reflecting an odd mix of amusement and fascination. "A rather peculiar object, wouldn't you agree?"

The mention of the infamous chair, long said to be used to confirm the gender of newly elected popes, stirred Michael's interest. He had studied it in his religious history lessons, aware of its existence but never quite comprehending its need. Now, hearing the Holy Father mention it, Michael couldn't help but echo his curiosity.

"Indeed, Your Holiness," Michael agreed, trying to conceal his surprise. "It has always seemed an odd... precaution, considering the stringent requirements for the papacy."

Pope Ignatius chuckled, a warm, throaty sound that resonated in the quiet chamber. "Indeed, my son. It's fascinating, isn't it? Our Church, an institution built upon faith, relying on such a primitive, physical means to confirm the gender of its leaders. Almost ironic, wouldn't you say?"

"I suppose it is, Papa," Michael acknowledged, feeling a strangeness in sharing this unconventional perspective with the Holy Father.

"Yet," Pope Ignatius continued, his gaze growing distant, "in light of Pope Joan's tale, the chair takes on a whole new meaning. It's no longer just a bizarre relic from our past but a stark reminder of our Church's fear and denial of the feminine strength and leadership. And since the first recorded mention of it is in 1099, not long after Pope Joan's reign, it could easily have been a result of her papacy that instigated its creation and use. This chair could very well be additional proof of her legitimacy, since one cannot image another reasonable use for it."

His words hung in the air, their profound implications echoing the sentiments voiced by Pope Joan herself, recorded in her diary.

"Yes," Michael responded, captivated by the Pope's insight. "It seems the chair is as much a symbol of our past shortcomings as it is a challenge for us to create a more inclusive future."

Pope Ignatius nodded, his gaze meeting Michael's. In his eyes, the priest saw a reflection of the path they were about to tread—a path leading towards understanding, acceptance, and hopefully, a revolution that the Church desperately needed.

In the soft light of the chamber, as the echoes of their conversation danced with the shadows, the significance of the Stercoraria Chair became evident—it was not just an artifact of an antiquated practice, but a symbol of the Church's journey from regression towards progression.

CHAPTER
THIRTY-FIVE

The sun had sunk beneath the horizon, the encroaching darkness shrouding the sprawling complex of the Vatican. In the shadowed corridors, the echo of a single set of footsteps reverberated off the grand arches and high ceilings. The figure moved with purpose, a sinister elegance in each step. It was Cardinal Bennett Dreyfus, a long-standing pillar of the Church and a *papabile* of formidable stature.

His journey led him to a secluded courtyard, its tranquility a stark contrast to the turmoil within Dreyfus's heart. He sank onto a cold stone bench, his mind embroiled in a battle between regret and ambition. In the silence of the night, the cardinal confessed his sins to the stars, the unblinking witnesses of his guilt. Yet, even as he laid bare his culpability, Dreyfus knew he would still do whatever he must to ensure his survival.

He had played his hand in the treacherous dance with Lord Pelham, but he was a chameleon, a master of adaptation. He would blend back into the heart of the

Vatican, biding his time within the hallowed halls. For now, he would don the cloak of humility, of penance, his actions cloaked under the veneer of servitude to the Church.

As the days turned into weeks, Dreyfus had already melded back into the tapestry of the Vatican, his past indiscretions—only rumored, never proven—fading into oblivion. His cunning mind focused on the future, the chair of St. Peter firmly within his sights. His actions were now marked by a calculated caution, every step a careful move on the vast chessboard of ecclesiastical politics.

In the privacy of his chamber, the cardinal would often gaze upon the portrait of the Vatican, the towering obelisk in St. Peter's Square casting a long, ominous shadow across the piazza. It was a stark reminder of the power and influence within his grasp, a visual promise of a future under his papacy.

The Vatican, unbeknownst to its inhabitants, was on the precipice of a new era, one even more daunting than the upheaval foisted on the Church by Pope Ignatius. The specter of Cardinal Bennett Dreyfus, cloaked in the vestments of the pope, loomed on the horizon. His ascent to the throne of St. Peter would not just signify a change of guard, but the dawn of a chilling era under a man who had learned to master the art of survival. His reign would be one marked by change, by progression, but at what cost, only time would tell. For now, Dreyfus lay in wait, his sinister ambitions concealed within the deepest recesses of his heart, biding their time to rise.

∾

In a quiet corner of the Apostolic Palace, Michael and Hana found a few precious moments of solace. Their hands were entwined, an island of warmth amidst the sea of uncertainty. The air was thick with the weight of what was left unsaid, their hearts beating in a rhythm that spoke of hope, anticipation, and a certain quiet joy. This was their first chance to be together since Pope Ignatius's groundbreaking Apostolic Constitutions had been announced.

The news of the papal mandate permitting priests to marry had felt like a gust of fresh wind sweeping through the ossified traditions of the Church. They had not spoken of what this could mean for them, their future remaining a subject touched upon only in abstract terms, but the glances they exchanged, the shared smiles, the charged silence spoke volumes.

Their whispers and soft laughter felt like acts of defiance, tiny rebellions against the solemn hush that had settled over the Vatican. They were expressions of hope, of life persisting amidst the shadow of mortality that loomed large.

This intimate interlude, however, was abruptly shattered by the sudden arrival of a Papal Gentleman. His countenance was grave, the lines of his face etched with concern as he relayed the distressing news: Pope Ignatius had collapsed, his life hanging by a thread.

The news hit Michael like a physical blow, the joyful bubble they'd inhabited punctured by harsh reality. Hana gave his hand a firm squeeze, a silent promise of support, her eyes mirroring his fear and dread. With a nod to the Papal Gentleman, he rose, their shared warmth still lingering as he rushed out, his heart heavy but resolved.

Arriving at his father's bedside, the magnitude of the moment was not lost on him. The pope, his father, lay there in a state of vulnerability, his breaths shallow and strained. A poignant silence filled the room, laden with the imminence of loss. But as Michael clasped his father's frail hand, a flicker of hope ignited within him. Even in the face of sorrow, they had accomplished so much. Change was afoot, and with it, the promise of a future brimming with untold possibilities—possibilities that his father, in his infinite wisdom and love, had set in motion.

CHAPTER

THIRTY-SIX

T he clock in the pope's quarters struck midnight,
its somber chimes echoing through the
hallowed halls of the Vatican's Apostolic Palace.
Michael Dominic, the son of Enrico Petrini, now Pope
Ignatius, sat in silence by the man he had only recently
come to know as his father. Behind them, along the
bedchamber walls, stood high-ranking cardinals, hands
clasped in silent prayer.

The pope's once robust frame was now a frail shadow
of its former self, as the ravages of time and illness had
taken their toll. The faint perfume of incense hung in the
air of the dimly lit room, casting a solemn, almost ethereal atmosphere. The room was silent, save for the steady
beep of the heart monitor and the quiet murmurs of
prayers whispered by the few cardinals present, close
friends of the pontiff.

Michael's heart was heavy with the weight of loss
and regret, not only for the impending death of his father
but for the time they had missed out on as father and

260

son. Enrico Petrini had been his mentor since birth, and his mother, Grace, had been Petrini's *inamorata* for a brief time, culminating in Michael's birth. The truth of their relationship had been a secret, known only to a select few, until two years ago. Now, it seemed cruel that fate would reunite them, only to snatch away what precious little time they had left.

Tears welled up in Michael's eyes, blurring his vision, as he reached out to clasp his father's withered hand. The man who had been a pillar of strength, a beacon of hope for millions, now lay dying. The heartache was over-whelming as Michael struggled to come to terms with the inevitability of his loss. He glanced around the room, dimly lit by the flickering candles casting shadows on the walls, and his gaze fell upon a photograph from long ago.

It was a picture of three young men, standing tall and proud in their military uniforms. Enrico Petrini, Pierre Valois, and Armand de Saint-Clair. The Maquis. The French Resistance. The memories rushed back, and Michael's heart swelled with pride as he recalled his father's tales of heroism and camaraderie in his youth.

Enrico Petrini had been a man of action, joining the French Resistance at the tender age of 17. Alongside Pierre and Armand, he had risked life and limb, fighting tirelessly against the oppressive Nazi regime. The three friends had shared many triumphs and tragedies, forging a bond that would last a lifetime. And it was during those tumultuous years that Enrico's faith in God was truly tested, ultimately leading him to devote his life to the Church.

After the war, Enrico had pursued his theological studies with the same passion and determination he had displayed in the trenches. With a keen intellect and an unwavering devotion to his faith, he rapidly rose through the ranks, making significant scholarly contributions to the Church. His seminal work on the intersection of faith and reason, *Lumen Fidei et Rationis*, had earned him widespread acclaim and respect among his peers.

Michael knew that he had been truly blessed to have a father like Enrico, a man who had managed to balance his profound faith and commitment to the Church with his role as a loving and caring parent, at least in these final years since telling Michael the truth. The bond between them had only grown stronger over those years, a testament to the depth of their love and understanding.

As Michael sat there, reminiscing about his father's life, he felt the weight of his own grief bearing down upon him. The tears he had tried so valiantly to suppress now flowed freely, coursing down his cheeks as rivers of sorrow. He could not bear the thought of a world without his father's wisdom, his guidance, and his love.

Michael leaned forward, his voice barely a whisper, as he began to pray. It was the prayer of Saint Ignatius of Loyola, the patron saint of Pope Ignatius, whose name his father had chosen upon his ascension to the papacy:

"Take, Lord, and receive all my liberty, my memory, my understanding, and my entire will, all that I have and possess. Thou hast given all to me. To Thee, O Lord, I return it. All is Thine, dispose of it wholly according to Thy will. Give me Thy love and Thy grace, for this is sufficient for me."

The words seemed to soothe Michael's anguished heart, as he found solace in the knowledge that his father's life had been a testament to the power of love and faith. Even as the darkness of death encroached,

Pope Ignatius's legacy would endure, a beacon of hope for generations to come.

In that moment, Michael felt a sudden warmth envelop him, as if he were wrapped in a loving embrace. He looked down at his father's face, now peaceful and serene, and knew that he was not alone in his grief. Pierre Valois, long since passed, and Armand de Saint-Clair, who himself was facing his last days, were there in spirit, standing alongside their brother-in-arms, their comrade, their friend.

As the first light of dawn crept into the room, Michael could no longer hold back the torrent of emotions that threatened to engulf him. His sobs echoed through the chamber, a raw expression of his grief, his love, and his gratitude for having been blessed with such a remarkable father.

A sudden change in the rhythm of the heart monitor caught Michael's attention. The once-steady beeping had become irregular, and he knew that the end was near. He reached out to take his father's hand, feeling the papery thinness of his skin as he clasped it gently. The cardinals' prayers intensified, their murmurs rising in a crescendo of supplication.

Pope Ignatius's eyes fluttered open for the briefest of moments, and in that instant, their gazes met. Michael saw a glimmer of recognition in those fading eyes, a spark of the love that had been denied them for so long. A tear escaped Michael's eye and slid down his cheek as he whispered, "I love you, Papa."

The pope's lips moved, barely perceptible, forming the words "I love you." Then, with a final breath, Enrico Petrini, Pope Ignatius, passed from this world. The heart monitor flatlined, a seemingly distant sound in the solemn silence.

Michael's heart ached with a pain that threatened to consume him, but he knew that his father's spirit lived on, not only in the hearts and minds of those who had loved him but also in the teachings and wisdom he had imparted. In that moment of profound sorrow, Michael made a silent vow to honor his father's memory, to carry on his legacy, and to live a life guided by the love and faith that had defined Pope Ignatius.

And as the sun began to rise, casting its golden rays upon the Vatican, Michael Dominic, the son of Enrico Petrini, stood tall and resolute, his tear-streaked face reflecting the determination of a man who would not let his father's light be extinguished. The world had lost a great leader, but the seeds of love and faith sown by Pope Ignatius would continue to grow, a testament to the indomitable spirit of a man who had touched the lives of so many.

EPILOGUE

The long shadows of the evening cast a spectral hush over Vatican City, the day's fervor giving way to the quiet pensiveness of twilight. Within the hallowed silence of St. Peter's Basilica, two figures moved through the nave, their steps echoing gently off the ancient stones.

Michael and Hana, hand in hand, walked side by side, their hearts heavy with a melancholic blend of loss and fulfillment. Pope Ignatius was no more. His spirit had quietly slipped away hours ago, leaving behind a legacy of change that would reverberate through the centuries.

Hana turned to look at Michael, his eyes reflecting the flickering candlelight, dancing with a myriad of emotions. He looked back at her, his gaze carrying a shared sorrow, yet holding a glimmer of hope and anticipation for what lay ahead.

"He did it, didn't he?" Hana whispered, her eyes misty. "He changed the world."

Michael squeezed her hand gently. "Yes, he did. And he left us with a duty to carry forward his work. To keep changing, to keep evolving."

In the hushed tranquility, they stood together in silence, lost in their thoughts. They mourned the passing of a great man, remembered his indomitable spirit, and contemplated the path that lay before them. They were both soldiers of faith, called to serve in different ways, yet united in their quest for truth and love.

As the bells tolled the end of the day, Michael turned to Hana, the shared understanding between them deepening. He gently tugged her towards him, enveloping her in a comforting embrace. Their hearts beating in synchrony, they found solace in their shared loss, their shared mission, their shared love.

"Are you ready for this, Hana?" he asked, the gravity of their shared path hanging between them. His voice was low, layered with the remnants of the day's sorrow, but laced with an underlying current of resolve that was undeniably Michael. His eyes, filled with a blend of determination and softness, held hers, inviting her to step into the journey that lay ahead. "Are you ready to walk this path together, to face whatever comes, and to shape a future that we can only dream of?"

Hana looked up at him, her gaze steady in the twilight, and in that moment, she was acutely aware of the depth of her love for this man standing before her. It was a love that transcended ordinary boundaries, a love forged in the crucible of shared experiences, battles fought side by side, and secrets unearthed. It was a love born out of respect, admiration, and a shared purpose that had pulled them together against all odds.

With all the conviction in her heart, she reached up to

caress his face, her fingers lightly tracing the outline of his features imprinted in her memory. She felt him lean into her touch, his eyes closing momentarily as if imprinting this moment into the recesses of his mind. "With you, Michael," she whispered, her voice carrying a blend of resolve, love, and a promise for the future. Her words hung in the air, echoing the vows of an unwritten contract of the heart. "Always."

As her lips met his cheek in a tender kiss, it was as if all their shared past, the trials, the victories, and their shared vision for the future, culminated in that simple act of affection. It was a confirmation of their unspoken pact, a signal that they were ready to face whatever lay ahead, together. For in their unity, they were stronger, and with their shared love, they were invincible.

Above them, the stars twinkled, as if winking at the promise of a new era. Their journey was not without challenges, but in the face of adversity, they had each other. In their unity, they found the strength to carry the torch of change, for the Church and for the world. And in the soft murmur of the Roman night, their shared heartbeat wrote the closing lines of an epic saga and began the prologue of a love story that would span the ages.

∽

FICTION, FACT, OR FUSION?

M any readers have asked me to distinguish fact from fiction in my books. Generally, I like to take factual events and historical figures and build on them in creative ways—but much of what I do write is historically accurate. In this book, I'll review some of the chapters where questions may arise, with hopes it may help those wondering where reality meets creative writing.

PROLOGUE

Owing to the fact that there are no contemporaneous accounts of Pope Joan during her lifetime—and the only known accounts of her emerged some four centuries later—much of what we know about Joan Anglicus, if she did in fact exist at all, is presumed, and what appears here was extracted from the few resources available on her. Keep in mind, too, that the Church was the custodian of most knowledge then, and most certainly all books, and thus controlled how history was recorded and what records were kept. A female pope would have not been something the early Church would have heralded, much less acknowledged.

The earliest known written account of Pope Joan was made by a Dominican friar named Jean de Mailly in the thirteenth century. He included the story in his "Chronicle of Metz," which was a compilation of historical events and legends. Other medieval chroniclers, such as Martin of Opava and Vincent of Beauvais, also wrote about Pope Joan in their works. However, it is unclear if these accounts are based on any historical facts, if they were passed down through oral legends, or if they are purely fictional.

Too, Pope Joan—or at least a female papal image— has figured prominently in tapestries and tarot cards since the early Middle Ages.

CHAPTER 1

The Codex Anglicus is a product of my own imagination, but it worked out ideally for the story. However, the Codex Vaticanus does exist, and its descriptions as discussed are all factually supported.

CHAPTER 3

Old English—or what was known as the Anglo-Saxon language during the Middle Ages—was the lingua franca of the era and has been translated as best as possible here.

· · ·

CHAPTER 5

The Lady Chapel of Sherborne Abbey does in fact have four stones engraved with the virtues of the Virgin Mary. As far as I know, they do not recede with pressure, as I've added that bit of magic along with the secret compartment beneath Lady Margaret's tomb.

CHAPTER 7

The papal monogram coinage shown here is a genuine artifact and could possibly be the actual coin issued for the reign of Pope Joan (as Pope John VIII) were she to be found as legitimate.

CHAPTER 8

Here I have stuck as close to documented history as possible, weaving the fabric of Pope Joan's life with actual people, places and events of the ninth century. Her son Gregory—whom I have named here fictionally—becomes the Bishop of Ostia at the same time a real Gregory became Ostia's bishop. This real bishop was named by the real Pope John VIII who served the Church at this time. I have established that Joan's lover, Cardinal Alexander Rossini (another real person), honored his paramour by taking her own regnal name when he rose to become Pope John VIII. The names and timing were simply too compelling for me to ignore, further blurring the lines between fact and fiction.

And in fact, Pope John VIII is rumored to have been poisoned and then clubbed to death in the 9th century. He served as Pope from December 14, 872, to December 16, 882. However, historical evidence on the circumstances of his death is not clear, and the accounts of him being poisoned and subsequently beaten to death remain unverified. The details of Pope John VIII's death have been the subject of speculation and sensationalized stories throughout history.

CHAPTER 15

It is unknown whether or not the Vatican possesses a Shard of the True Cross or a Thorn from Christ's Crown of Thorns. Many churches and religious institutions around the world claim to have fragments of the True Cross or the Crown of Thorns. These relics have been venerated by the faithful, and often they've been passed down through the centuries. However, their authenticity is difficult, if not impossible, to verify.

One notable example is the Crown of Thorns at the Notre-Dame Cathedral in Paris. It is considered the cathedral's most precious and revered relic. It was originally held at the Basilique Sainte-Chapelle in Paris, which was built specifically to house it, before it was moved to Notre-Dame in the 18th century.

Moreover, prior to the Seventh Crusade, Louis IX of France bought from Baldwin II of Constantinople what was venerated as Jesus' Crown of Thorns. It is kept in Paris to this day, in the Louvre Museum.

Relics that are purported to be from the True Cross are found in many places. The Church of the Holy Sepulchre in Jerusalem and the Basilica di Santa Croce in Gerusalemme in Rome are two places that claim to possess fragments.

In any case, it's always good to remember that the importance of these relics comes primarily from the faith of the believers who venerate them, rather than their historical authenticity.

CHAPTER 33

In the pope's signature, the customary "PP" is an abbreviation for "Papa Pontifex," which is Latin for "Pope" and "Pontiff," respectively. Therefore, when a Pope appends "PP" to their name, it serves as a formal title and a reinforcement of their role as both the Bishop of Rome and the head of the Catholic Church.

CHAPTER 34

There is actually a most unusual "Pope's Chair" from the Middle Ages—whose origin and purpose is murky, if not unknown—as pictured in this chapter.

Its official name is "Sedia Stercoraria" and legend has it that—in order to prevent another female pope from sneaking in—the newly elected pontiff had to sit on it while a deacon put his hand under the chair and verified that the new pope had masculine attributes. Once the sex of the subject was confirmed, the deacon proclaimed: "*Duos habet et bene pendentes,*" Latin for "*He has two and they dangle nicely.*"

Though there is some controversy about the chair's origin, most scholars—the same ones who deny there ever was a Pope Joan—eschew the chair's legend. See more at Wikipedia.

AUTHOR'S NOTES

Dealing with issues of theology, religious beliefs, and the fictional treatment of historical biblical events can be a daunting affair.

I would ask all readers to view this story for what it is —a work of pure fiction, adapted from the seeds of many oral traditions and the historical record, at least as we know it today.

Apart from telling an engaging story, I have no agenda here, and respect those of all beliefs, from Agnosticism to Zoroastrianism and everything in between.

~

Thank you for reading *The Confessions of Pope Joan*. I hope you enjoyed it and, if you haven't already, suggest you pick up the story in the earlier books of The Magdalene Chronicles series—*The Magdalene Deception, The Magdalene Reliquary,* and *The Magdalene Veil*—as well as books featuring the same characters in the ongoing Vatican

Secret Archives Thriller series. Then look forward to more stories in this series as these same characters—and new ones—continue to hunt, find, and face the truths behind the mysteries of the past.

When you have a moment, may I ask that you leave a review on Amazon, Goodreads, Facebook and perhaps elsewhere you find convenient? Reviews are crucial to a book's success, and I hope for The Magdalene Chronicles and the Vatican Secret Archives Thriller series to have a long and entertaining life.

You can easily leave your review by going to my Amazon book page. Since Amazon doesn't allow review links to be posted in books, just search for *The Confessions of Pope Joan*. And thank you!

If you would like to reach out for any reason, you can email me at gary@garymcavoy.com. If you'd like to learn more about me and my work, visit my website at www.garymcavoy.com, where you can also sign up for my private Reader's List.

With kind regards,

Gary McAvoy

CREDITS

CREDITS:

Wikimedia Commons contributors, "File:Woodcut illustration of Pope Joan - Penn Provenance Project.jpg," Wikimedia Commons, the free media repository, https://commons.wikimedia.org/w/index.php?title=File:Woodcut_illustration_of_Pope_Joan_-_Penn_Provenance_Project.jpg&oldid=648987298 (accessed April 4, 2023).

Made in the USA
Columbia, SC
21 January 2024

30753511R00171